Assumptions and Carnations

To John,
you are part of
Cambridge — and that's
saying, *Satori*

Assumptions and Carnations

Simon Satori Hendley

Immanion Press
Stafford, England

Assumptions and Carnations
By Simon Satori Hendley
© 2006

Cover by Vincent Chong
Art Direction and Typesetting by Kid Charlemaine
Editor: Storm Constantine
Author photograph: Adrian Judd

Set in Souvenir

First Edition by Immanion Press 2006

0 9 8 7 6 5 4 3 2 1

An Immanion Press Edition
http://www.immanion-press.com
info@immanion-press.com

8 Rowley Grove
Stafford ST17 9BJ
UK

ISBN 190485334X
From Jan. 2007 ISBN 978190485334X

'For Adelle, for P. Marie & for Acanthamoeba'.

Chapter One
Belief and the Art of Car Maintenance

Enschol Bralcht had lost so very much; not just his memory but the things that go with it; friends, family, possessions, his life. He knew that he was dead and that he had finally bullied his way into some kind of resurrection, but beyond this the spiritual battle to keep his ego intact meant that he had discarded almost everything else. For instance, there was a part of him that kept nagging that his name was not Enschol Bralcht at all, but something more English and mundane, but he had forcibly to ignore this because the myth of Enschol Bralcht, master-magician and resurrectionist, was strong and simple and necessary to stop him being just another complicated set of events and emotions that would fall apart with the next gust of astral confusion.

His body, if it could be called such, was made from belief. Yes, I think it could be called a body: it walked like a

7

body, breathed like a body, touched and tasted like a body and its lack of stability; its tendency to disappear when not in full view should not lead us to question its corporeality. There is a trick to changing energy into matter and nobodies into bodies. It has something to do with an input of energy and a force of will and Enschol forced all his energy into his physicality, until it gave him a migraine in a head that had only just come into existence. Poor Enschol Bralcht: it would not get any easier until he killed somebody.

Enschol Bralcht first manifested amongst the trees of Wandlebury: a spiritual nexus for the Cambridge New-Agers since the old ages. In the sixteenth century, Cambridge students had been banned from joining the rituals and festivities at the old Iron Age fort. There may or may not be burial mounds, carved chalk figures of giant horses and ghosts amongst the trees. Enschol Bralcht's own brand of weirdness was not out of place here. He gazed across to Cambridge with a ghost-sense that twitched something in his head but could not really be called sight, or smell or sound or taste or touch. He was searching for another nexus, but this time with people. He could not make plans as such, as too much of his conscious brain was fixed on the task of keeping his consciousness together. Instead, he had a series of instincts that he trusted to follow to reach his goal. His mind made up (and kept together) he began to walk to the town, sometimes with his feet in contact with the ground. Sometimes friction and gravity did not quite agree with him and his legs made walking motions in the air with no forward propulsion at all.

No one in his right mind would pick up a hitchhiker from Wandlebury at night. You could pick up bad feelings from Wandlebury at night. You could pick up a nasty cold, when the mist that had stubbornly refused to accept that the old marshland had been drained millennia ago, settled in the dips below the Gog Magog hills. But you did not pick up hitchhikers. Thomas Hypolite was a philosophic danger-man. If you said that something could not be done, he believed it was his duty to test the hypothesis. He was the sort of person who would pick up a hitchhiker from the depths of hell and go out of his way down the back streets of purgatory to drop him off at his house... so long as the hitcher did not mind Tom's Bob Marley CDs played at full volume for 'mechanical reasons'.

'Thank you, for stopping', said Enschol Bralcht as he opened the car door and let the Reggae and warm air out.

'PARDON', said Tom,

'I SAID THANKS', shouted Enschol Bralcht.

'NO WORRIES', said Tom. 'DO YOU LIKE BOB MARLEY?'

As has been previously mentioned, Enschol Bralcht's personality was a fragile thing, recently built out of convenient myth and self-belief. He did not know if he liked Bob Marley, just as he did not know if he had a favourite colour, or where he came from, or how many were ten, or if planets were a good idea, or much else besides the primacy of his being. He was alive. He would stay alive. All else was simply details of no importance.

'YES', he said.

'WHERE DO YOU WANT TO GO?' (An awkward question to someone with such a limited knowledge of geography).

'INTO TOWN? …I think…' (Bralcht's voice tailed off).

There was a period of silence, or there would have been if Mr. Marley hadn't been so keen to confess to 'SHOOTING THE SHERIFF…' at the top of his lungs. Enschol Bralcht idly picked up and examined the CD case. It said that he was listening to 'Bob Marley and the Wailers'. Something in his new being found that amusing and he laughed a little to himself: trying on a new emotion to see how it fitted.

'EXCUSE ME…' he asked as politely as he could shout, 'WHY IS THE MUSIC SO LOUD?'

'HUH?'

'I SAID, WHY IS THE MUSIC SO LOUD?'

'…OH, I'VE GOT TO PLAY IT THIS LOUD FOR MECHANICAL REASONS.'

'WHAT?'

'…DO YOU HEAR A SLIGHT RATTLING FROM THE ENGINE AND A CLUNKING SOUND WHEN I CHANGE GEAR?'

'NO. I CAN'T HEAR A THING.'

'SEE... NO WORRIES!'

Every time Thomas Hypolite looked ahead at the road he had a feeling that the man in the passenger seat wasn't there and some voice in his head queried whether he had picked up a hitcher at all. Only when he turned his head to look at his passenger did it become clear to him that the hitchhiker did exist and his unease was due to some defective dope that he had recently brought from his local dealer. Tom had to smoke dope for 'cultural reasons'. Two generations ago the Hypolites had come to England to help the post-war economy and the Jamaican blood was running thin in Tom. He needed his ganja and his Marley like an intravenous drip to keep his levels up and prevent him from becoming just another lazy English post-grad in baggy t-shirt and faded jeans. At night, when the dope could play with an imagination unfettered by waking reality, Tom dreamed of turning Caucasian, putting on a suit and becoming a bank manager. He would wake up sweating and light up a joint in shaky hands.

'MY NAME'S TOM.' shouted Tom.

'ENSCHOL BRALCHT', shouted his slightly invisible passenger.

'...ARE YOU ROMANIAN?' Tom had never been to Romania; just as he'd never been to Jamaica, but he thought the name sounded as if it must come from somewhere

11

further east than Norwich and Romania was as good a guess as any.

'YES' said Enschol Bralcht with the conviction of a man who would have agreed to being French, Welsh or Chinese with equal credibility.

Enschol Bralcht eventually got out of the car somewhere along the Cambridge ring road. He felt, or smelt, or touched, that the nexus was close by. It wasn't a church. The thing he was looking for did not look like a mosque, sound like a temple or taste like a synagogue. The nexus was something different and therefore of more use to Enschol Bralcht: a centre of belief, nebulous enough to be manipulated. He did not know it yet but he had struck a rich seam of pagans.

Michael was the owner of a large house of indeterminate age in a suburb of Cambridge that still thought it was a village. His house, however, ever since his breakdown and phoenix-like reinvention, was also his business. He was 'The Guru of Cherry Hinton'. He had altered his environment to become a Mecca for the spiritually disenfranchised. As well as regular meetings of like-minded souls in a local pub, he also liked to open his house for financially and spiritually rewarding 'Retreat Weeks', where he would share his knowledge of man and the universe in return for a share of his students' wealth. He was neither a greedy man nor a charlatan, but he owned a big house with big bills and his beliefs were flexible enough for him to have a realistic view of mammon.

Michael ran something called 'The Fellowship of Cambridge Pagans'; a group of a dozen or so like-minded people who pensioners and the Press would still refer to as hippies. But now, for want of a better description, they agreed to be pagans. Michael himself had periodic crises about the word, since occasionally he would read a book that pointed out that a lot of his rituals and practices dated only as far back as the 1960's: the pagan dawn was but a fine line on the temporal horizon, and he was just a backlash to his own Christian upbringing. However, a cup of herbal tea and a new book about the handing-down of Celtic witchery through some unexplainable dynasty would cheer him up again and the word that was etched on a brass plaque on his door would stay. Depending on the situation and the current state of his library, Michael was 'a bit of a Buddhist', 'a bit of a Wiccan', 'a bit of a spiritualist', or 'a bit of a warlock'. Jesus Christ (a derided and deniable figure amongst the pagans) once called one of his disciples 'a rock' upon which he could build his church. If one of Michael's spiritual masters were to describe him, they would probably have likened him to 'a bouncy castle'. To his credit, he seldom forced his ideas down anyone's throat and anyone who knew him described him as 'a bit of a nice bloke'.

When his wife left (with a Presbyterian, whatever one of those was), he set about redesigning his house along similar lines to the redesigning that was going on inside his head and heart. At the back of the house was something he called 'The Entropy Room'. At the front he had knocked through a number of walls to form one big bare room filled with hundreds of bowls full of candles and nothing else. The effect during the evenings was wonderful with a thousand wicks giving a temple-like aura to the room. During the day-time it was a bit too obvious that his friends and guests were not as fastidious as he would have liked, as the light-bearing contents of the bowls were invariably cluttered with an alarming number of cigarette butts and bottle tops.

The kitchen looked like it had once had an owner who had cared for it but now had to satisfy itself with an existence as a canteen or tofu-burger bar. It looked dejected. The kitchen had been designed for modern executive living and the assortment of paper bags full of fruit, vegetables, plants, rubbish, wood chippings, gravel, muesli, lightbulbs, bottles, and fir-cones that sat on every flat surface lent the room an atmosphere somewhere between chaotic charm, cold-war air-raid shelter and garden shed. (Michael's garden shed, on the other hand, was well lit and well stocked with tools and carpentry equipment and had a second room completely full of balsa wood.) From a black and white tiled hallway, a dramatic attention-seeking staircase led to an upstairs landing from which Michael's bedroom and its seven simple guest-room clones sat with only four or five bathrooms for company.

Michael's greatest and worst creation was the garden.

It was his greatest because it was so beautiful and thoughtful and humorous. He had designed something called a pot garden. It was an exercise in control as a paved area was given life only where Michael wanted it. The plants were all grown in plant pots of different sizes, heights and widths arranged meticulously to feel as if man had learnt something from nature and had created something separate but in accord with it. What made his garden special, though, was his choice of plants: no garish hybrids, no exotic garden-show fancies - he grew weeds. Although this was true it was not the complete truth. Michael did not just grow weeds as other gardeners did, (unwelcome between flowers, surreptitiously nestling in the cracks in the paving, persistently sticking up amongst the gravel, fighting trowels and chemicals), he grew them with purpose and in an isolation that allowed you to appreciate them, probably for the first and only time, as individual and beautiful parts of nature. Stinging nettles were kept in large round terracotta tubs: raised up to just below eye height to display the lush green leaves and the deceptively stroke-able fine fur upon the stems. Dandelions were grown to incredible sizes, one per pot, with the 'clock' of seeds standing proud in the centre or that big orange solar disk that any shop-brought plant would be proud of, were they not from so common a stock. These dandelions, highlighted in their single pots did not look so common. A wooden arch with its feet sunk into two large pots of cow parsley was consumed by voracious bindweed,

15

the epitome of 'healthy growth'.

Everybody loved the garden. Even those who accidentally brushed past the thistles, brambles and nettles, and stung or prickled their skin into nervous life, confessed to loving its whimsy. The only person who did not fully enjoy it was Michael. To him, it was the worst thing he had done. Its existence was a penance to him. One of his friends once told him that, despite Michael's claims that it was an example of his respect for all things, it was in fact, an example of Michael's obsession with rejection. If it showed respect for all things why had he carefully picked his shunned flora; why were there no flowers? He had found his spirituality during the dark period when his wife had left him. His friends and students were all oddities and rejects in the normal world. It all made sense and it all seemed to belittle his achievements and goals. He was not a good man intent on being an example of love for the world: he was a broken man collecting broken things. The garden was a symbol of this and Michael used it to deflate his ego whenever a success had filled it with too much gas.

Enschol Bralcht found all this out in a whirlwind tour of the house, once he had got past the guard at the door with his clever reasoning of the password:

'Are you here for the Week's Retreat?' said Michael.

'Yes' said Enschol Bralcht, and he was let into the house and into Michael's confidence.

Some of Michael's pagan friends held secrets like currency. They believed in 'hidden knowledge' and 'buried truth', and any knowledge or truth that they happened upon they immediately rehid and reburied close to their chests, up their sleeves and out of bounds. Michael, however, was a river way. He could not hold on to anything for long; beliefs, ideas, knowledge or truth flowed through him and over him and past him, and when Enschol Bralcht found out everything in his tour, he found out *everything*. Even Michael's fears and faults were admitted quite freely to a stranger, who looked as though he had only just learnt to smile that day and didn't want to over-practice, and had the unnerving ability to disappear when not in your full view.

Michael took Enschol Bralcht into one of the guest rooms. 'What do I call you? What's your name?' enquired the host, affably.

'Enschol Bralcht'

'…are you Italian?' asked Michael. He was quite good at guessing where people came from, or thought he was.

'Yes', said Enschol Bralcht in a matter-of-fact way, but he did not elaborate any further. There was a pause whilst Michael waited to be told something like '…I come from a little village named…in the hills of…have you ever been to…it's lovely at this time of year.' Michael was told no such thing.

'Um…this is where you will be staying…'

'What will we be doing whilst we stay here?' said the mock Italian.

'Um…well a bit of relaxation, a bit of realisation, a bit of psychic attunement, some spiritual healing and we'll end with some life affirmation and general consolidation rituals.'

Michael turned his head away momentarily and was left with the feeling that he was quite alone in the room and talking to himself. He turned his head back and saw his new European friend had a decidedly blank expression on his face…

'Would you like to see the syllabus?' he asked.

Downstairs, the other guests were already starting to introduce themselves to each other. They carefully tried small talk about the weather and then attempted pleasant conversation about their beliefs and magical or spiritual achievements, but these all sounded suspiciously like boasts and so eventually the conversation returned to the low-brow basics that all strangers are left with: football and television.

'Did you see Coronation Street, last night?' asked Lynn with the quick desperation of someone who felt the awkwardness of talking with people she hardly knew. Lynn was a neurotic. At various times (and depending on medicine company trends) she had been on Valium, Diazepam, Mogadon and Prozac. She had broken down and got back-up again so many times that God had withdrawn his warranty on her. She had lived with abusive men. She had seen loved

18

ones die. She had her excuses. But still no one could say that she had a reliable temperament and it was a shock to her friends (among whom Michael was included) when she became a counsellor. In this role, she looked after people who were having problems. She was undoubtedly a sensitive soul, and she was qualified to speak about most of the horrors that life could bring, but this was still a little too close to the cliché: 'The blind leading the blind'. In fact it went beyond that cliché to become 'The screwed-up guiding the screwed-up'. Lynn knew Michael and Bog, the ex-biker with the silly name, who she turned to now in the hope that he would pick up the subject of 'Coronation Street' and begin a fully-fledged mature conversation with it.

'No.' said Bog 'I can't stand it.'

Bog had skin like Stilton cheese with pale blue graffiti in random squiggles across his body. At one time, these would have been dark and threatening tattoos of skulls and women and bikes, but age or weathering had faded them to the colour of varicose veins. He was short but stout enough to be menacing when he stared you in the eyes. Even when (as was more common) he could only lift his stocky neck up enough to stare at you in the nipples, it was a stare of intensity and broken-bottled promises. Bog had a sullen nature that belied his true friendliness. His many friends all suspected that his sullenness began five years ago when he had had to sell his beloved Norton and buy a more practical four-wheeled vehicle. This off-hand psychoanalysis was backed up by the fact that Bog still remembered the model, number plate and chassis number of his old bike but referred to his car as 'a four wheeled vehicle'. He frequently had to walk back home from pagan meetings in the pub: not because he was too drunk to drive but because he had lost his only means of transport home. No matter how hard he tried (and to be honest he never did), he could not remember the car's number plate, shape or even colour. In fact, the only reason that he had begun to improve in his 'four wheeled vehicle recognition skills' was because for the last four months he had kept a bale of hay on the back seat. Why there was a bale of hay in the back of his car, no one knew and it had now been there so long that no one asked him. Bog had a good reason, though.

Gavyn and Violet knew Bog and vaguely knew Michael. Violet wanted to become Buddhist, although she did not really know what this involved. Gavyn suspected that Violet's vision of Buddhism as a peaceful faith of wise shaven-headed sages did not quite match up with the wars and ignorance that existed in Buddhist states as much as anywhere else. He wanted to be Christian. He thought that anything so hated by his friends and colleagues must have something in it, and if there is one thing that all the pagans hated, it was Christianity. The couple had to be careful about how vehemently they expressed their conflicting beliefs, but whilst talking in spiritual generalities they usually agreed and formed a hybrid religion that was not a million miles away from Gnosticism. Whilst not at pagan retreats, Violet was a teacher at a local school. Gavyn was once a computer engineer, but was made unemployed a month ago and now had no excuse but to join Violet amongst true believers of whatever.

Then there was the stranger: stranger to everyone but Michael, who met him on a park bench when the stranger started to talk to him about his magical powers. The stranger's name was Kelly Martin and the four others decided that they did not particularly like him within the first minutes of meeting him. Kelly had a mental condition that probably would be recognised as a fully-fledged, benefit-claiming, sympathy-grabbing disease in the future. Perhaps it might even be called 'Martin's Syndrome'. At the present time, however, you would have to describe it as an inability to interact with other people along normal social patterns. There was no subtlety or diplomacy in his interactions. He just butted into conversations with his strange non-sequiturs. 'I once conjured a demon into the material plane,' he would say to no-one in particular, 'but I don't know where it went. I think it got lost and settled down in the airing cupboard... it always seemed much hotter in there than it should have done and my boiler was never the same...'

Upstairs, Enschol Bralcht was reading a five page description of the five days that the group would be staying together. He was taking his time to read it, because like every other skill, the resurrectionist had to remember how to read before attempting this. Nothing came easy. He was so afraid of corporally disintegrating, that most of his energy was used to think about the reality of Enschol Bralcht and only the little dribble of energy that was spare could be devoted to other tasks. Poor Enschol Bralcht.

There was a ring from the doorbell. Michael had managed to change the chime to sound more like a peel of church bells and so most people in the house were a little confused by this noise. Michael, however, indicated to Enschol Bralcht and walked downstairs to answer the door.

Standing on the doorstep outside Michael's pagan palace was an impatient old man, usually called 'Old Dan'. In the plum of his youth he had been an attractive six foot tall university team rower — now he was a prune. He was small and wrinkled and sour, but he knew more about the psychic history and ghost stories of Cambridge than anyone else. Einstein's Theory of Relativity states that there is no fixed point in the universe and all measurements are relative to the observer's own moving point of reference. There is, however, a more popular theory of relativity that has no named proponent but is just as important to our view of the universe. This theory states that perceived time is relative to the amount of fun you're having, the amount of pain you are in or the effect that the moment will have on the rest of your life. The next few minutes seemed to last forever for Dan.

In the front room the stilted conversation slowly lost its stilts and found its feet (and people learnt to ignore Kelly Martin). By the time Enschol Bralcht and Michael came downstairs they were talking intelligently and freely about complete rubbish. It was a dangerous conversation though because it had turned from football and soap operas to the difference between men (Y chromosomed football fans) and women (double X soap addicts). Gavyn, one nervous eye on his partner, addressed the group: 'Why is it that men who hate women are called misogynists, but there is no comparable word for women who hate men?'

'What about misanthropist?' said Strange Kelly,

'But that means hating all mankind. It's not gender specific!'

'Hhmmm', said the collective male psyche.

'Hhhmmm', said the suspicious female psyche awaiting the next part of the argument.

'…Is it…?' said Gavyn with an apologetic glance at Violet, 'because there are no women who hate men… or is it that women's hatred of men is so natural and acceptable that there is no word for it?'

There was a pause where tigers stalked. Then, Violet, her partner's equal, pantomimed a look at Bog and Kelly and Gavyn and said, 'I don't hate men… I just hate all of you!' and everyone laughed.

And then there were church bells. Most people

ignored them thinking that they came from a church, which as a symbol of the Christian faith was something that they had programmed themselves to ignore. Bog, however, had stayed at Michael's before and headed for the door. Kelly followed him because Kelly had to do something.

Enschol Bralcht and Michael came downstairs, Michael leading the way. He opened the door, saw Old Dan and said, 'Hi'.

Old Dan looked behind Michael at the figure on the stairs. He looked at Michael and at Bog and at Kelly who stood in the hallway and, with an expression that could have been pity or anguish or the beginning of a heart attack, fell to the floor, managing only to dribble the word 'Bollocksh…' from a mouth curled down to one side as if he'd just been to the dentist and his lips had yet to wake up from the anaesthetic's magic.

Everyone stood still for a relative moment before Bog awoke from his paralysis and rushed to Old Dan's side shouting, 'Phone an ambulance. Michael, you idiot, phone an Ambulance.'

But Michael had another idea. The non-decisive, non-confrontational Michael stood upon the stairs as if they were an orator's platform and in a voice that was not quite his own said, 'No. We'll drive'. An intelligent idea, whoever it was who said it. Although Addenbrookes Accident and Emergency ward was but a couple of miles away, for an ambulance to be dispatched to Cherry Hinton and make it back to the hospital, it would have taken longer than for Michael and party to make it there... even though they didn't have any blue flashing lights or sirens or even, for a short panicked minute, a car.

'What do you mean you don't know where you parked?'

'I mean I don't know where I left the damned vehicle', said Bog in an irritated mumble like thunder on the horizon.

'OK,' said Michael, 'help me with the garage door and we'll get my car out.'

And so they did, and Michael's old manager-mobile crept backwards out of the garage. The cardboard boxes that had been put 'out-of-the-way' on its roof came falling in little avalanches to the sides and preceding the great twelve cylindered behemoth was the blue cloud of exhaust: the expected herald for such an under-used memento of Michael's previous working life. Bog thought it was lucky the thing started at all.

Once the car had been extricated from its resting place, Michael tried the windscreen wipers, slowly remembering what all the little extra buttons did. The blades squeaked across the glass and wisps of dust were thrown to either side. Michael tried the lights. He didn't need them. Now that the screen was dust-free he could easily do without lights... it was coming up to midday. Michael, however, just had to try the lights, as a small piece of memory buried under the boxes in the garage of Michael's mind recollected that the lights were important. These were the reasons he had brought the car in the first place all those years ago, when he had been an executive and married and stupidly content with his lot. The lights, when the correct button was pressed, rose majestically out of the bonnet, and when he pressed the button again they'd descend again into the smooth lines of the dusty, rusty but still proud executive toy. Now, however, as Michael pressed the button, one and one half lights emerged from the bonnet, the motor made a shunting noise, followed by a clicking noise, followed by a silent lack-of-noise, and one and one half lights remained above the bonnet: one whole and one squinting eye stared into the garbage of the garage, like an old lecherous man winking at a young boy.

Michael, Bog and Kelly bundled Old Dan into the back of the car. If questioned about it at a later date, none of them would be able to confess to seeing Enschol Bralcht at all during this time. They hadn't noticed him since Michael had taken control of the situation. However, quiet and unassuming as he was, Enschol Bralcht must have been helping in some capacity.

Back at the house, the rest of the party were beginning to feel uneasy and a little rejected. They had been abandoned by their host and were left in an unfamiliar house for who-knew how long. Since they had yet to reach such social niceties as exchanging mobile phone numbers and Michael's mobile (the one telephonic link between all of them) was sitting mockingly on a small table beside the door, they had no way of contacting the others and no idea what they should do now. Luckily, despite their attempts at breaking out of their culture and establishing themselves as freethinking individuals, culture is a creature older and bigger than the individual and it cannot be destroyed. The 'British resolve' therefore leapt in to prevent panic spreading. Gavin stood up, cleared his voice with a throaty cough and heroically asked if anyone wanted a cup of tea. This was a great plan. Everyone agreed. This was the answer to all of life's problems. The making of tea allows you time to think, the drinking of tea has a psychological calming effect and the symbology of tea reassures you that the world has some stability, and no matter what technological or sociological changes take place, there will always be infusions of leaves in hot water.

Gavyn went into the kitchen and regretted his decision immediately. It took him two minutes to find the kettle: one hundred and twenty seconds of pushing aside the clutter on the various work surfaces before he revealed the holy vessel that he sought. The water was easier; it came from a tap. The taps were situated above the sink. The sink was that place in the kitchen where all the dirty pots, pans and plates had chosen to die; sinking slowly in grey fetid water. Tea bags. Where the hell, would Michael keep tea bags? Gavyn searched in places that should never be searched: in the cupboards of the damned and the shelves of perdition. He eventually found some in a pot marked

'Coffee' which led him, logically, to track down the sugar in the pot marked 'Salt'. The milk (soya-based, non-dairy white liquid) was, somewhat surprisingly, found in the fridge. Gavyn had completed his task and strode back into the front room beaming with pride, like a knight back from a quest.

'Any biscuits?' said Kelly.

Chapter Two
Drowning Wishes

It would be three hours before Michael and the rest of the Pagan Fellowship returned and Gavyn, Violet, Lynn and Kelly were all relieved to see their host again. As well as having an altruistic concern about the old man who had collapsed on the doorstep, they were starting to fear that their retreat might never happen. Michael calmed them all down and explained that Old Dan was probably going to be in hospital for a week at least and that the retreat would continue as planned, but it would be nice if people could take a few minutes out of the schedule each evening, to visit the old man.

Michael took a sip from the teacup Gavyn had passed him (in the three hours, Gavyn had braved the kitchen on several occasions and was now quite blasé about the dangers involved). He sat down on the floor and explained the rules to his guests. Michael's mild mannerisms meant that the rules that he thought he was fervently imposing came out as recommendations, but none-the-less, he asked if they could keep the noise down after twelve o'clock. His neighbours still had jobs, after all, and were merrily rat-racing towards either a fruitless retirement or a heart attack. He explained where the toilets were and explained the layout of the house, including the mysterious Entropy Room at its rear. As he knew some of the guests quite well, he was happy to joke with them or insult them as part of the explanation. He looked around the room and said, '... Bog may annoy you with his bluntness', (Bog shrugged), 'Sometimes Lynn might seem too much of a hippy,' (she mocked anger at being insulted and then smiled at Michael to continue), '...and sometimes I may bore you to death, or be too preachy or something... When this happens, you go to the Entropy Room and you break things. I don't know why this helps, but it does. Perhaps mankind is designed or destined for destruction. Whatever the reason is, we are genetically coded to receive a real catharsis from destroying things. Once you've smashed the place up a bit though, and you're feeling healthier and calmer, I ask you to go to the shed at the bottom of the garden where you'll find the plans and materials for remaking the furniture and ornamentation. Don't worry, it's not difficult... it's all made of balsa wood and I've remade the room four times over since I came up with the idea: I just expect everyone to take some responsibility for their actions...'

And everyone agreed.

And so Monday evening continued as planned: the group meditated for half an hour, the group performed a visualisation ritual (dedicated to the health of Old Dan), the group ordered Vegan pizza and then the group talked philosophy, football and television into the early morning, drinking wine and smoking something that Kelly had got from 'Dealer Tom'. Although nothing that occurred that evening would make it into the local newspapers, some occurrences do need elaborating.

For the meditation, Michael put on a CD called 'Pan-pipes and Whales' and instructed the group to sit cross-legged (or full lotus if they could), straight backed, eyes-shut and concentrating on nothing-in-particular. If anything in particular did pop into their minds, they were to ignore it until the next anything came along and pushed it out of the way. Michael was good at meditation. He hadn't quite got to a stage where he could remove all thought from his head but he had enough trust, experience and character to let random thoughts cascade through his brain unhindered by consciousness. However, during this meditation session one thought would not cascade through. A dark thought, like a half remembered message to yourself to switch the cooker off, nagged at him. The thought had no form or detail to it, but as nonsensical as it might seem, the thought had a personality.

Thus, for Michael, the wine and dope part of the evening was far more relaxing than the meditation as the flow of conversation helped scour away the dark blot in his mind.

Lynn also felt a little uneasy from the meditation, but said nothing.

Gavyn and Violet felt comfortable enough.

Kelly felt enriched.

Bog felt happy, because he usually used meditation as a way of daydreaming about the days that he used to bike down to the South coast, swerving through traffic like a predator through grazing animals — and who's to say that this wasn't the correct approach?

Enschol Bralcht however, used the meditation time for more important things. As everyone had their eyes shut, 'The Italian Guest' tried to ascertain which body was likely to contain the most energy but the least will power. He didn't even know he was doing it.

Kelly had his uses. He would babble on about angels and animals and zoos and Zanzibar and all manner of things in between. He would never seem to be fully following anyone else's conversation and his contribution to a discussion usually had no bearing on the subject at all, but he could roll a mean spliff. Enschol Bralcht watched the odd little man's fingers like you would watch a concert pianist's. It was poetry in action: the kissing and arranging of the papers, the caressing and positioning of the tobacco and the grass, and then the deft folding of the package into something smokeable. The wine flowed and the narcotic smoke provided a welcome gauzy haze to protect late-night eyes from the bright candles. They were talking about Zoroastrianism at about two o'clock in the morning; it was a good subject as everyone had an opinion but no-one had any in-depth knowledge to get in the way of speculation and romantic posturing. Then, all of a sudden Kelly (who had not been paying much attention to the conversation as usual) said 'Hombadiddley?'

'What?' said the others, speaking as one.

'Hombadiddley?' (It was obviously a question.)

'What are you talking about?' said Bog.

'You said Hombadiddley?' said Kelly, inferring 'Why did you say Hombadiddley?'

'No, you said Hombadiddley!' said Bog.

'No, I don't mean then, I mean before.'

'What?' said everyone.

'Who said Hombadiddley?' asked Kelly, showing something approaching accusatory anger.

'You did' said everyone, still confused.

'No. Before I said it, someone else said it,' Kelly explained agitatedly.

33

'Hombadiddley?' asked everyone.

'Yes.'

'Why would anyone say Hombadiddley?'

'I don't know…I didn't say it.'

'Well, what does it mean?' asked Bog.

'I don't know…one of you said it,' insisted Kelly.

'Hombadiddley?'

'Yes,' said Kelly. 'Someone said Hombadiddley.'

'Before you said Hombadiddley, someone else said Hombadiddley and you want to know why someone said it?' clarified Gavyn, who was keen to move on to a more sensible conversation.

'Yes' said Kelly.

No one remembered saying the word. No one knew what it meant. No one could think of any word or set of words that might have sounded anything like 'Hombadiddley'. It wasn't Violet, as she was asleep on Gavyn's shoulder, and it wasn't Enschol Bralcht, because he had already gone to bed. He had taken a puff of Kelly's cigarette and then had just disappeared without saying goodnight (poor Enschol Bralcht). It wasn't anybody. Kelly was so annoyed that the others were insinuating that he was lying or stoned or mad that he had to go into the Entropy Room and break some things. Meanwhile, the others spent half an hour debating on what the word might mean and how to spell it. By the time Kelly came back in, they were able to announce that Kelly's new word had a silent 'w' and

should   be   spelt
'W...H...O...M...B...A...D...I...D...D...L...E...Y'.

'Whombadiddley,' muttered Kelly as he wandered upstairs to bed.

'Whombadiddley!' cheered the others and waved him goodnight.

The next day, after hangovers and during breakfast (tea and muffins rustled up by Gavyn the Brave), Michael explained that today magical realisation techniques would be experimented with and they would have a road trip. This was on the understanding that Bog would help ferry some of the group in his car, (Bog grunted approval), and that Bog could remember where he had left his car, (Bog made a less favourable noise). The plan was to go to Grantchester.

Grantchester was a theme park of old middle class England: it was too expensive for anyone to live in, and had been trapped in the 1930's since the 1930's. It was visited by coach loads of tourists who wandered around cooing at the thatched cottages and dribbling into the dark English ales that were available in the English theme-pubs. Like all good theme parks, though, just because a cynical mind could see it for its fakery, it did not diminish its appeal. It was, after all, beautiful: so sodding beautiful it hurt any sensitive young psychic to go there. The spirit of England...not the real England...but the green-tinted, slow-timed, civilised spirit of Middle England morris-danced into your soul and played with your nostalgia switch. The character and caricature around which the theme park was built was no big-eared mouse. Rupert Brook was the face on the pub-signs, in photos on walls, postcards and historical plaques: Rupert Brook, who died during the Great War before his image could age. Forever young, the poet's intelligent search for the Classical beauty of nature led Virginia Woolf to call him, and his entourage who came punting up the Cam to see him, 'The Neo-Pagans'. This was perhaps a coincidence.

The Orchard was the theme park's Middle English fast food stall. It served fresh cream cakes and teas rather than burgers and hotdogs, and you could eat at your leisure amongst the fruit trees, the blackbirds and the opportunist wasp nests. It was here that Michael read from a couple of disparate books: first from a dry Crowlian text on the relationship between nature and the wild magic, secondly from Rupert Brook's homesick poetry for the naiads of the River Cam and fauns of the Grantchester water meadows, and thirdly from his Retreat Syllabus, which connected the two to come up with today's activities. He explained how Rupert Brook was at the core of Tuesday's work and how poets created something out of nothing. They linked things that were un-linked, crafted ideas and realities from ephemeral words and gave us all something to believe in.

'Something out of Nothing.' Enschol Bralcht knew a little about poetry.

It was at Grantchester, that Bog finally confronted

Enschol Bralcht about something that had been nagging at him since they were first introduced. Bog had this feeling that something about Enschol was false, and in the meadows, separated from the others, he asked Enschol Bralcht what he wanted to ask him: 'You're not from Italy are you?'

'Yes,' said Enschol Bralcht.

'...You're German aren't you?'

'Yes,' Bralcht said, and Bog walked away; happy to have uncovered this great secret.

Down in the meadows there was more flowing wine, (Bacchus was toasted liberally), and paper and pens were handed out. Michael explained that they were going to be communing with Brook's naiad directly. They were to write down their dreams and their aspirations on the little bits of paper, whilst pin-pointing in their mind the image of a liquid maiden; lithe, with muscles rippling rhythmically, hair like green water-weeds that stretched far behind her, glittering smile, glittering eyes, fluid of motion and thought. Everyone concentrated: a dualist effort, as the pictorial part of their brains focused on the image, whilst the intellectual part put together a respectful and truthful wish and then tried to command a pen to write neatly on the paper without being able to ask the arty part of the brain for help. This was more difficult than it seems and most people's handwriting for this exercise had a most naïve appearance. This was perhaps appropriate as it bound the activity with that of a child writing for the first time to Santa Claus for a bicycle, a computer or for Mummy and Daddy to stop fighting. This was all about primal wants and base needs. It was a difficult exercise but most agreed that it was worth it.

Enschol Bralcht kept quiet, however, because he had not written anything on his paper. This was not because he had no aspirations, wants or needs: his undead nature was powered by such strong forces. He hadn't written anything because concentrating on a wet woman in a stream, writing down a wish list and being Enschol Bralcht, all proved too distracting for him and he was starting to visibly fray at his edges.

Next, Michael showed them how to make paper boats from their pieces of paper. This was the sort of trick school children had been taught to do before television came and robbed them of such magic. It was an origami of such beauty and simplicity that it used to appear regularly in 'Rupert the Bear' annuals, and the whole idea fitted seamlessly with the slow flow of nostalgia that was the essence of Grantchester. Michael had chosen the paper specifically because of its absorbency, so that when the craft were placed gently into the River Cam they floated with the grace of miniature swans into the central flow, travelled two or three feet down-river, soaked up the water, lowered their sails, lowered their masts, and lowered everything else as they slowly sank down to the naiad's waiting arms.

There, beneath the surface, the naiad would know who had been naughty or nice and grant them their wishes according to her own capricious whims.

After this exercise, the group spent a while there; lying back in the grass, arranging themselves around the cowpats. Beside them, the river that had swallowed their wishes continued its nonchalant meandering to the sea. It was another idyllic moment at the local idyll. For most of the time Michael held court. He didn't bully his way to dominate a conversation as Kelly did, but instead, people naturally looked to him for acceptance when they talked. Lynn, as the only single female, seemed particularly interested in what he had to say: an interest that was probably piqued by the fact that Michael didn't really say much. The only person less talkative than Michael was Enschol Bralcht, who may have said something that day, but no-one could remember what it was.

Violet had a lot to say about hypnosis and symbolism as she was currently reading a book on the subject, and Enschol Bralcht was most attentive as she spoke. Bog and Kelly had an argument about Kelly's abilities to hypnotise people. The argument got quite heated and Bog would later say that he 'didn't know what got into him,' but the others all agreed that Kelly was being particularly annoying that day.

Eventually, however, the crickets and grasshoppers heralded the going down of the sun and a chill mist came in like modesty, to hide the cows from their ankles downwards.

The group decided to go back to Cherry Hinton via

Addenbrookes to see their fallen comrade. The nurses however were not happy to see six oddly dressed people trampling cowpats along the hospital corridors. Some nurses sometimes saw seven people in the group, but the gentleman in the black but nondescript clothes kept wandering off and was obviously keen to stay at the back of the group. Six or seven, however, made no difference to the Matron or Nurse-in-Charge who came out of her office at a commanding pace and stood in front of them like Hippocrates' very own bouncer. She explained firmly but calmly that perhaps a few of them, (maybe one or two of them), would like to visit tomorrow when the patient would be more coherent. There wasn't anything else to be done but to accept this pronouncement, but having spent fifteen minutes finding a parking spot in the hospital car park, Michael and Bog were not happy about this. Others however were less upset about this decision and Enschol Bralcht, still trailing at the rear of 'the magnanimous seven', was practicing his smiling again.

When the two cars left for Cherry Hinton, their spaces were taken by two more cars and on a screen in the security department, two red blips turned blue and blue blips turned red. This was a small detail of little importance to most people, but not necessarily to James 'Jimmy' Chamberlain, scientist, student, security guard, technician and coffee junkie. He was collecting data. He was watching. He was analysing and calculating. He thought of himself as the least spiritual being in Cambridgeshire and was proud of this. He thought he was practical and logical and that these abilities would help him explain every phenomenon that the world had to offer. Poor Jimmy: his philosophy was naïvely wandering through the jungles of circumstance, where a predator in black clothing was waiting with an immature grin.

Later that night, a rainstorm hit Cambridgeshire and everyone stayed up into the morning hours to watch the lightening play across the sky in a Faraday Ballet. The rhythm of raindrops beating on roof tops, so fast that you could only comprehend it as one constant sound, was hypnotically relaxing and Michael explained to everyone a theory of his. 'I read a book once...' he began, 'that explained that the Chinese believed that every body of water contained and was governed by a dragon. The dragon's size and importance was decided upon by the size and importance of its domain: so the huge dragon of the Yangtze would be kowtowed to by lesser river dragons, but in turn it would respect the power and authority of the dragon of the South China Sea.' Michael had a good audience who were tired from a long day of boat-building and were content to listen to a storyteller's voice as it fought for respect with the sound of the storm.

'That means...' he continued, 'that every lake, river, stream and pond has a controlling spirit and in every single individual raindrop there is curled up a homuncular dragon; a brief ruler of his little domain until it must admit subservience to the lord of the puddle or the drain or the river.'

Lynn put her hand out of the open back door and caught a raindrop, or twenty, in her hand and stared at it for a while, thinking of dragons and of Michael.

Chapter Three
Don't Drink The Coffee

The next day was a wet Wednesday. The storm had subsided but had given way to the grey drizzle that, since Caesar's scribes had first landed on these Isles, would always be described as typical British weather. This was unfair: Britain has a variety of climates, seasons and atmospheres and the literary linkage to drizzle is surely just lazy journalism, or perhaps jealousy, as writers from foreign countries are used to the tedious monotony of constant sunshine. But to the pagan group, the weather meant that any planned excursions had to be put off until another day.

Enschol Bralcht thought back to the time when he had first entered the house and had been handed a syllabus of the week's activities. This document bore no similarity to the actions of the past couple of days, nor did it seem likely it ever would do. He had been deceived. There was not a plan: Michael made up each day's activities on an apparent whim. Enschol Bralcht found that he did not like being deceived. His mood became blacker than the weather and his presence seemed less real as his anger grew more intense. Enschol Bralcht would have his revenge though and Michael's laid-back liberal non-predictable, non-existent plans would be a tool for it. But now was not the time. Now poor Enschol Bralcht was disappearing from people's minds, their peripheral vision and their breakfast table, and in an effort to calm himself back into reality he half-floated, half-walked to the Entropy Room to concentrate his form into enough fleshy matter to destroy balsa wood furnishings. Whilst the others ate their muesli, sounds of swearing and smashing came from the back of the house and when Enschol emerged with real sweat upon his real brow, he was met by Michael, who knew what was wrong with his Italian guest.

'There'll be other days to see the beautiful English countryside,' he reassured Enschol Bralcht. 'There'll be other days'.

If Bog hadn't bellowed a 'Listen to this!' that summoned everyone's attention at that very moment, someone would have seen an expression emerge on Enschol Bralcht's passive face: an expression of disdain, despair and icy hatred. But nobody noticed.

'Listen to this!' repeated Bog and rustled the local newspaper he held to indicate that he was going to quote from it. He had been absent-mindedly reading the second-hand bike pages and an article about the Radiology Department at

Addenbrookes, when he found himself reading the obituaries. 'Do any of you remember the road-doctor?'

'Who?' said a collection of voices.

'The old guy in the fluorescent coat who used to walk up and down the A14 making notes on a clipboard and collecting squashed animals in plastic bags'.

'Yeah, I know the man' said Gavyn, and most of the others made similar sounds of agreement.

'Who?' said Kelly,

'He was a bit like Marigold, the guy in Norwich, you know, the guy with the rubber-gloves on who directs traffic whether it needs to be directed or not; a 'local character', you know the sort?'

'Who?' repeated Kelly annoyingly.

'Let me read this to you,' said Bog and he rustled the paper again as punctuation. 'Professor Lewis began his studies in sociology in the dark days of the 1980's, when sociology as a profession was seen as a joke. He knew that the society that he studied thought that sociology was a subject that academics did when they weren't good enough to study 'proper subjects' and it has been said that this hurt him, personally. He was a diligent man, an intelligent man, and he studied a society that did not appreciate his endeavours.'. Bog was now 'reading' with only cursory glances at the newspaper. He had been involved in pagan communities for many years and had some experience of speaking rituals, sermons and spells for audiences both

45

physical and metaphysical. He knew therefore that the printed words were less important than the feel and flow of the story and if his biography of the road-doctor was more elaborate than the original journalist intended, then it did not concern Bog's current audience.

'His initial papers, on modern fairytales and urban myths, were respected within his field: new insights on old tales, old roots revealed beneath new legends. He studied the rise of the football hero and the decline of the warrior gods.

'In his later years, now a white bearded professor with eccentric twitches that his students laughed about behind his back, he studied strange road kills. He started with the raw data: the odd things found in the hard shoulder, in the central reservation and pan-caked between the cat's eyes — animals native and exotic, plastic oddities, wooden trade gifts and metal offerings to motor deities — shredded tyres to haulage giants, spilt loads for the angels' share and mixamatosisised rabbits offered upon long transport altars.

'He persisted with this throughout his career. He wrote a lot of more orthodox papers on teenage pregnancy, the traveller phenomenon and drug use at university, but in the evenings after work he could be seen wearing his reflective yellow coat, hiking along the verges of A-roads for more data for his growing files. Every so often he would try to organise his data into some sort of order. He would try to show the pattern of wealth distribution of the country by the types of road kill and litter that could be found in an area. He would journey outside his field of study to consult with biologists to compare notes on regional speciation. He would desperately try to find a pattern within an overwhelming number of occurrences. It was suspected that his frustration and countering obsession for the subject, was the cause of his increased shaking and his slurring stammering speech.

'For a time the professor was admired within the scientific community for his physicality. Although a little stooped with age, his passion for walking long stretches of roadway kept him alarmingly fit and able to throw paper balls at sleeping students right at the back of the lecture theatres. However, his stoop became more pronounced, his shaking unstoppable and his speech incomprehensible. Professors and post-grads rallied together to fill in for the lectures that he could no longer take and helped write his ideas into coherent papers, and it is at this stage the defendants crossed the line of compassion and law.

'It is alleged that the sociology professor (still a giant's mind within his shrinking body) manipulated his colleagues into helping him. You must remember that his colleagues, men and women of academia, live their lives in the ivory towers of science and the arts. They have become separated from the rules and responsibilities of the rest of society. They even study society itself, as if they were outside it, looking in. Due to the nature of the court case, this journalist cannot say whether they did or did not consider the morality or legality of the situation, and it is saddening that an obituary must become marred by criminal proceedings.

'When the disease had rendered the sociology professor helpless the conspiratorial faculty helped him and complied with his final request. He was picked up, (he weighed little more than 60 lbs), and put in the back of the university's Transit van. The van was driven back and forth along a stretch of the M11 motorway at three o'clock in the morning, until they were sure that no one was directly following them. Then they tipped the professor out onto the road. A small bundle, the size of a deer or perhaps a large fox, he would become strange road kill: his small body ripped and flattened across the tarmac. Is this murder? Is this manslaughter? Is this recklessness to be called euthanasia? That is for a jury to decide. Professor Lewis's life ended in irony. The student became the subject of the study: a fitting end perhaps, but lacking a moral or a happy-ever-after: a very modern fairy-tale.'

There was a few minutes' silence: out of respect for the dead, out of reverence for an odd story and the surprisingly eloquent storyteller, or perhaps out of a lack of anything to say? But when the silence passed it became clear that the rain would not and Michael began busying himself for the day ahead.

Wet Wednesday was not to be wasted. Michael

gathered the group together in the front room and got them to move all the pillows and candles to the walls to reveal a forgotten expanse of floorboards. Everyone was shocked at the space this seemed to create from out of nowhere; here was housework made miraculous, humble cleaning turned to thaumaturgy. Michael glanced at Violet conspiratorially and, as the rain streamed across the windowpanes behind him in homage to waterfalls, Michael, the very spirit of a Taoist adept, announced that today they would be learning some elementary Tai Chi.

They took the training very slowly: appropriately enough as Tai Chi always appears to be Kung Fu committed in slow motion. Bog had a theory that Tai Chi was invented by a particularly sullen Shaolin monk who was told he had to wash the temple steps once he had finished his martial arts practice. The monk, a stroppy teenager, Bog supposed, then took it upon himself to slow the movements down to a crawl until the elder monks had to wash the steps for themselves and he was sent to bed without a bowl of rice, to sulk and listen to modern chant-music on full volume. Violet, who had studied Ta Chi for about three months and was therefore the expert of the group, explained that it was more like a 'moving meditation': this might explain the difficulties the group had.

As explained earlier, Bog used meditation as an excuse to daydream about motorbikes, but his unconventional mindset was probably not the problem. Bog's problem with Tai Chi was more likely linked to his body. The graceful movements of long limbed Orientals were reduced to a clumsy waving of limbs from a stocky Occidental trying hard not to fall over. The damp weather was also playing havoc with his bad leg.

Gavyn, although he kept the fact secret to everyone including Violet, was not a natural meditator. He was too protective and secretive to let his mental doors and windows open. He'd had a bad experience once whilst undergoing hypnotic regression and wasn't going to be seen metaphysically naked in public again.

Strange Kelly was shockingly good at Tai Chi. He was either a natural at it or had studied before. He was however hindered by Enschol Bralcht who was moving in the most mysterious way beside him.

Logic said that there was enough space in Michael's front room for everyone to be able to move, stretch and balance without coming into contact with anyone else's body. Everyone had started the session by stretching their arms out as far as they could and making sure that they were no longer in reach of anyone else. No one could possibly hit anyone else and distract them. It could not happen. Logic however did not meet many individuals like Enschol Bralcht. The Russian, (Kelly was convinced that Enschol Bralcht was Russian), kept hitting him in the face and the stomach and the leg. Poor Enschol Bralcht. His mind, stretched thin whilst trying to ascertain the psychic state of his colleagues, could not maintain the standard configuration of his own body. Bits grew longer as he stretched them. Elbow and knee joints, that evolution had methodically designed to work in certain predictable ways, began to plot anarchy in the power vacuum that Enschol's absentee mind had created. Enschol Bralcht became a slow moving epileptic contortionist and no one in the room was safe from a slap in the face. This was so off-putting that there were even times when graceful Violet started moving like a puppet with all of its strings cut, although she would later complain that during these periods she didn't 'feel like herself'.

The Tai Chi session ended at lunchtime, and whilst Lynn made a refreshing but foul-tasting natural lemonade for the group, Kelly sulked his way to the Entropy Room to break some things. He was muttering mild curses to Enschol Bralcht before he got there, so when he found that the Russian had not yet had a chance to rebuild the furniture and he had nothing unbroken to break, he began to swear loudly. His only recourse was to break the bits of balsa into smaller bits until he was covered in dust and splinters and the room was so full of wood dust that it would have made your eyes itch and your chest spasm. It took Lynn to finally calm the little man down and coerce Enschol Bralcht and Kelly Martin to shake hands and make friends. She made them both drink from the same glass of lemonade as each other, as a symbol of how they were united in their purpose of seeking knowledge and understanding. As the two unlikely colleagues went off to the shed to rebuild the Entropy Room, Gavyn burst into laughter. He alone amongst the group had realised the true symbology of Lynn's cup-sharing consolidation ritual — there just weren't enough clean glasses in Michael's kitchen to go round.

In the shed Kelly and Enschol began to pick out the sheets and lengths of balsa and the tubes of glue and the furniture blueprints and the tools, when Kelly got distracted. He had just lifted up a huge (but lightweight) panel of balsawood that even now he could perceive was a coffee-table just-waiting-to-happen, when his vision snagged on a large item buried at the far end of the shed, beyond the balsa forest and amongst the papers, the boxes, the disused lawn-mower and the rusting bicycle frame. He walked carefully through the clutter to examine the item and was shocked to discover a casket: a metal coffin resting against the wall. In theory, modern pagans are the most accepting and un-judgemental people in the world, with such a broad background of beliefs and practices that nothing shocks or disturbs them. In practice, however, a human being is a human being and despite Violet's hopes of Buddhist transcendence, very few of us ever lose our preconceptions. Kelly's preconceptions included one that said that anyone who had a coffin in his shed must have an interesting reason for putting it there, and he could think of no good reasons and plenty of bad ones. Perhaps Michael was planning to kill himself: he was suicidal...a particular well-planned suicidal...capable of premeditative self-destruction... although how he was going to bury himself after he had killed himself and placed himself in his coffin, Kelly could not fathom. If Michael was capable of killing himself, however, then must he not be capable of killing other people? Perhaps he was planning murder rather than suicide? Perhaps he was a particularly well-mannered serial killer, who instead of chopping up or dissolving his victims in acid, liked to give them a full ceremonial burial beneath the stinging nettles and thistles and paving slabs of the back garden? Kelly's imagination had left the house of facts and was moving through the gears on a fast-lane to horror fiction. In an effort to reverse this trip to hysteria, he started to consider (with more hope than faith) that this might just be a rather badly chosen design for a storage locker or bookshelf or something. He shifted a pile of papers from in front of it and opened the lid, to reassure himself. The inch-long spikes that lined the casket where far from reassuring. This was not a burial casket; this was a torture device and Strange Kelly was beginning to feel strangely nervous of his host. 'It's always the nice ones...' he said to himself.

In the Entropy Room, Kelly and Enschol Bralcht worked surprisingly well together: Kelly couldn't stop talking (perhaps as a way of covering up his new fear and doubt about Michael, or perhaps because Kelly was like that anyway). Enschol Bralcht on the other hand was reluctant to open his mouth and the two men complimented each other. Enschol Bralcht's unconscious mission to learn about the spirit, soul and minds of the group was made deliriously easy by a man who would not do anything else but talk about his own thoughts and experiences. Enschol Bralcht was so happy that he even tried his smile again, although when Kelly stopped gluing together two pieces of wood to ask what the matter was, Enschol Bralcht gave up his experiments with facial muscles and began to concentrate on what was important.

Kelly worked (and talked) tirelessly and there were moments when he went into a meditative state, or so he thought, because every now and then he would wake from a shallow daydream to discover that he had completed another chair or sideboard without any apparent conscious effort. These were the moments when Enschol Bralcht would fade to a near translucence. These were the moments when Enschol Bralcht would go exploring where he was unwanted and uninvited. These were the moments when Enschol Bralcht, resurrectionist and psychonaut, would trespass into Kelly Martin: an uneasy journey.

Enschol Bralcht's odyssey, from the shores of his own unnatural being and into Kelly's labyrinthine psychoses was a frightening experience and there is little in the realms of metaphor or simile that can describe the downward spiral through the layers of excuses, tissues of lies, deceits, self-deceits and infantile and implacable truths. Poor Enschol

Bralcht. This was no walk in the park. This was not a roller coaster ride. This was a hard and perilous slog and the few minutes that Enschol Bralcht spent exploring Kelly's complex psyche belied the epic quality of the journey. Imagine a single Kelly Martin story: for instance: 'I once levitated four foot in the air, whilst I practiced channelling with the Golden Dawn'. Kelly believed eighty percent of this story, and felt guilty about exaggerating sixty percent of the tale, and knew exactly why he could not tell the full truth, but had forgotten more than a third of the experience, because he was half hypnotised and half drugged at the time, and the majority of the audience who could collaborate the story, were drunk and delirious. Enschol Bralcht had only been Enschol Bralcht for three days; the strain of being Kelly Martin for two minutes was incredible. This would be the second time in a single day that Enschol Bralcht would leave the Entropy Room with sweat on his brow.

'Are you OK?' asked Gavyn, showing his best concerned face, although not really listening for an answer.

'Whombaddidley,' muttered Enschol Bralcht with a sigh; as if it meant something.

Gavyn nodded sagely and continued munching on some toast that he had managed to cook in the unpromising environment of Michael's kitchen.

Michael had planned (as much as Michael planned anything),

to have a group photo taken on the last day as a souvenir of the joy and success of the bonds that the Fellowship of Pagans had made with each other, but whilst he had the group together, resting from the morning's exercises, and whilst the front room was tidy, he decided that the photographs should be taken now.

There was some unease about this plan. There is a dance that lies unshifting beneath the Western culture and to break it is a taboo. The dance has a rhythm and a beat and a name and today we call it 'false modesty'. This group was fuelled by ego. Each individual believed that they were better than the herd that surrounded them. Each individual believed that they were original and clever and wise in some way that others were not. Some, (like Enschol Bralcht), believed that ego is a power: a force to combat stubborn and passive nature. Some, (like Violet), believed that ego was a stumbling block: a shackle from which to shake free, in order to ascend to a higher realm. Everyone agreed on the importance of ego. Yet, here we are amongst the men and women of ego, pretending that their chance of immortality is a cup of poisoned wine. When Michael took out his camera, everyone stared at it like the magic box that it was and a dance began: every child of vanity pretends that being the subject of art and the centre of a portrait is far from their wishes and they only begrudgingly smile before the lens for the sake of the cameraman. Yes, there were exceptions and excuses. The women would not appear again until they had rushed for mirrors and lipsticks and powders, in fear for their beauty. Enschol Bralcht was reluctant to face the camera until he had re-established a memory to its usage: was it a toy? Was it a weapon? And Gavyn suspected that cameras conspired against him.

As they all meandered on their reluctant path to the front room, Gavyn claimed the position usually favoured by mysterious Mr. Bralcht. He was the last to enter the room and as they lined up in two self-choreographed lines Gavyn pushed his way to the back and slouched as best as he could behind Enschol Bralcht. He didn't like cameras...or more realistically, they didn't like him. They made him ugly. His nose might be bigger than average. His eyes might be closer together than a handsome man's, but surely he was not ugly. Paranoid, Gavyn would look in mirrors for the ugly man to show himself, but could not find him and although photographs showed someone similar to his mirror-self, something was missing; something that added a little handsomeness. He suspected that it was 'life' that the camera could not catch and, contradictory to the beliefs of the apocryphal primitives, the camera did not steal your soul. It could not even capture it for a split second. It showed no life, no spirit and no soul; nothing but ugly flesh.

Time seemed to flow like water from an English sky. Michael did not need to plan anything for the afternoon: the afternoon had plans of its own. People talked. People talked over cups of tea and coffee and occasionally the chatting became a lecture and everyone's particular interests came out. Teachers separated from students, only to merge again into a mass of friends and separate again in a different pattern. In this way, Lynn told everyone about Reiki: an American slant on a Japanese interpretation of Tibetan healing techniques. Violet was particularly interested. She'd studied a little about Tibetan culture and once went to a benefit concert to kick out the Chinese oppressors. Her faith in Japanese and American cultures was less than true, but then ideas have no geographic boundaries and cannot be held accountable for their origins.

Time kept flowing. No Canute could turn the tide, and afternoon became evening before anyone had even noticed. Certainly, it had come as a surprise to Michael who, encouraged by Bog, had discovered some homemade wine that had been 'laid down' in the cupboard underneath the stairs, ten years ago. The plum wine smelt of bile and could not be drunk without gagging. They had to tip two bottles down the crowded kitchen sink before they came across a vein of fine ten year old English pear wine: sweet like sherry, alcoholic like science-lab meths.

Thus when Michael remembered his promise that members of the group should visit Old Dan every evening, he himself was not in a suitable condition and Gavyn, Kelly and Enschol Bralcht were volunteered for the task. Meanwhile

Violet was taught Reiki by Lynn in the front room and Bog volunteered for the job of keeping Michael and his alcohol company.

'So you still have some sort of feelings for her?' asked Bog, incredulously.

'Yes. I guess so… We lived together for ten years and I can still see her standing in most of the rooms…'

'You're being haunted by her?'

'Well no, she's still alive and doing well, with a man called Tim, in Guildford,'

'But you're still be haunted by your ex-wife?' Bog repeated,

'Yes. I guess so.'

They talked about the bad times. They talked like the old friends they were: about Michael's slow and stuttering progress from married man to single man. Michael, (and most people his age), thought that there was something unnatural about this: men were supposed to be boys, grow to be young men and then at the correct juncture in their lives, marry and live together with their wives, happily ever after… like his parents… like everyone's parents.

They talked about screaming.

During a rough patch in Michael's marriage, whilst he and his wife were driving back from some argument-disguised-as-a-two-week-holiday-in-the-Lake-District, he found himself screaming at the top of his lungs. This had scared his wife and he had promised not to do it again in front of her, but still it had felt good. The problem was that in an over-populated country like Britain, where politeness dictates that raised voices are kept to a minimum, people don't scream enough. Even if you went right out into the Black Mountains of Wales to relieve the stress of your modern working life, you could not shout or cry to the heavens, for fear of some wandering hiker hearing you, confusing your cry of anguish with a shout for 'help!', and calling mountain rescue on his mobile phone. Then, when the helicopters arrived on the scene, you'd be likely to have all kinds of explanations to make.

'But the key to screaming in the modern world,' said Michael, 'is driving...'

What Michael used to do was take his big old car out onto a nice straight motorway and scream until his throat hurt beneath the din of the traffic; alone and unquestioned; shielded from the prying world in a cage of metal and glass. Michael believed this had helped him maintain a calm attitude during the long divorce procedures. He hadn't used the car for a while though. Perhaps he was getting better and didn't need to scream so much, but this confession left Bog with a disturbing image in his mind of thousands of car drivers with nowhere to go, driving up and down the motorways; screaming. The roads weren't over-crowded with commuters and people with important journeys and known destinations: the reason why congestion was increasing was directly due to the increasing stress-levels of society. The motorways weren't there as a transport system: they existed for a more metaphysical purpose: they were arteries of pain.

This talk (and the alcohol) were having a beneficial effect on Michael as much as any vehicle-related emotional outbursts. The thought that he was haunted by his ex-wife actually gave him hope. Michael was not very convinced about psychology. His generation not only believed in the permanence of marriage but also the 'sort-yourself-out' philosophy of mental health and he had no faith in psychoanalysis. But exorcisms, now there was something he believed in. There was a technique, a real and acceptable procedure, for removing unwanted essences. His problem had a solution. He had hope.

'So, let's do it...'

'Yeah,' said Michael.

'Yeah!' said Bog.

'What?!' said Michael.

'Um...let's hold an exorcism.'

'Yeah?!' said Michael.

'Yeah.' said Bog, and the timetable for the next evening was decided over the remains of the English pear and a cocktail that the two had concocted from a half-bottle of Vodka that they found in the kitchen and the only fizzy mixer they could find: a can of non-alcoholic Lager. They called their new creation 'Drinkable' and they laughed about it for some time. Then they stopped laughing and had another couple of Drinkables each and started laughing again, because they could not remember what they were laughing about...and they found this funny. This was a good night for Michael.

Lynn, standing by the doorway, having left Violet to memorise some simple chakras, found this incredibly endearing. Being a broken woman she had always been attracted to broken men, and Michael's confessions of guilt and loss about his failed marriage were sweet love-songs to her ears. She had come to the kitchen to make some tea for herself and Violet, but had stood quietly rapt in the two men's drunken conversation for the last five minutes; almost afraid to break the magic of the moment as stream-of-conscience babble came from Bog and Michael. 'Michael is a good man', she thought.

Meanwhile, Gavyn, Kelly and Enschol Bralcht were driving through the Cambridge traffic and thinking of Tai Chi. The Cambridge traffic system is surprisingly similar to Tai Chi. Cars move in careful dances, similar to normal transport systems, but slower and more methodical, as if practicing for some future time when they would be able to travel faster than 20 miles an hour.

If this was travel slowed to a meditation, then the parking at Addenbrookes was another type of mind-trip altogether. Buddhist monks repeat hand movements until they flow into mindless repetition and are called mudras.

Perhaps the twenty or thirty times around a car park in search of an unclaimed parking space could be seen as a ritualistic clearing of the mind, but if this was meditation, it was doing little to calm Gavyn down. He was driving Michael's large and unfamiliar car and although he had proved his bravery and persistence during his military campaign in Michael's kitchen, he was not pleased to find himself, once again, taken for granted and taking responsibility for his less able colleagues. Perhaps parking was indeed a meditation: after all, Gavyn hated meditation.

Eventually, they managed to find a space large enough to park in and, somewhere, a little red marker on a screen in the security block, (a Portacabin between the toilets and the car park), turned into a little blue marker. The programmer who had spent several days creating a program to make red dots turn blue was coincidently in the foyer when the three pagans entered the hospital. Jimmy Chamberlain was proud of the program that he had written, which would, he believed, allow the whole of Addenbrookes' parking system to be realigned along scientific principles to allow more cars to park in less space, faster. Jimmy Chamberlain was not so proud of his responsibility to tell idiot Luddite receptionists how to use the security cameras effectively. How he yearned for his under-graduate years when he could hang out with programmers and engineers and avoid talking with all these other inferior specimens. How he hated lowering himself to the position of 'a monkey with a screwdriver' just to pay his way through his post-graduate work. How he wondered why the security monitor at the front desk only picked up two people entering the hospital when there were quite clearly three.

Once the three people (or two people) had passed by, into the labyrinthine clean white depths of the hospital, and once Jimmy had finished telling Jane, (her name was written on the badge on her shirt), how to switch the monitor to show a variety of scenes from a plethora of cameras, (wishing all the time that her smiling, nodding and sawdust-filled head would snap off and a faster more able head would emerge from the stump), Jimmy ran back to the security block. His fingers rattled over the keyboard whilst his eyes scanned the monitors, flicking from one camera view to another. Each foyer camera showed the same thing: two people entering the building. One was a man, about five foot ten in height, with mousy-brown hair, a long nose and narrow face and the other was a shorter man, perhaps five foot five, balding, but the last remains of brown hair had decided to try to make up for its loneliness by erupting into chaotic flares from the sides and back of his head. To be fair to the small man, it must have been windy in the car park, because behind the two of them (in the place where Jimmy had seen the third man) the door stayed open for a few seconds, as if it were caught by a strong wind.

Jimmy's hands played over the keyboard some more, until he saw what he was looking for on the screen. The two men were walking up the stairwell to visit a friend in one of the wards. He followed them: not in a personal or physical way, but from the antisocial security of his security office using one camera after another as his eyes.

Gavyn and Kelly were oblivious to this. They were talking about monotheism and pantheism and whether you could believe in both at the same time. Gavyn argued strongly that Christianity was a pantheistic religion with a hierarchy of spiritually powerful beings (saints and angels) who were regularly placated in prayers to help mankind. He said that despite saying that there was one God and one God alone, its churches were littered with icons representing other god-like beings. He said it was similar to the way that the roots of Buddhism were profoundly atheistic, but gods slowly found their way into the religion as it spread through time and geography, and saints, angels and bodhisattvas were all gods by any other name. Whether Gavyn believed this was not relevant. Gavyn had just discovered that the best way to prevent Kelly from talking was to lecture him about something that *you* were interested in and to allow no room for him to issue forth an opening syllable. Kelly, meanwhile, waited his turn, patiently, to tell Gavyn about when he met God on a cliff-top in Somerset and how he had argued something similar to God at the time. He was so excited about what he was going to say that he stopped listening to Gavyn and was just nodding at what he thought were the right moments, waiting for a lull in the speech so that he could launch his own topic. Enschol Bralcht was quiet and brooding as always, but he seemed distracted today. His hawkish eyes kept looking at the security cameras as they made their way to Old Dan's ward.

Gavyn knew it had been a mistake to come as soon as he entered the ward. Dan was found fairly quickly, despite the hospital's best efforts of replacing his individuality with bland neatness, but Gavyn was not sure it was Dan, or at least not the whole Dan. He knew that cleanliness and a factory-like mass-production system must be used to keep patients as healthy as possible, for as little of the tax-payers money as possible, but he hated to see all these grey men, in their identical fading pyjamas, in identical uncluttered beds, lined up like graves in a cemetery. Dan, meanwhile, was not currently capable of expressing his individuality, even if he were allowed to. He was muttering and nodding and occasionally gave lucid words of thanks to Gavyn and Kelly but he couldn't really say much, because he wasn't sure where he was, or when it was, or why two people he once met in a pub during a pagan 'moot' (or 'meeting' as non-Pagans would call it) would come all this way to see him. Dan did not see Enschol Bralcht. Enschol Bralcht was either avoiding Dan or he was too busy looking at the security camera in the corner of the ward - a camera that had moved sympathetically with their entrance — a camera whose tiny motors were now whirring away to move a lens forward to focus in on some new items of interest that had entered the room.

Gavyn had no patience for embarrassing silences and agreed to go and find some coffee or tea for Kelly, Enschol Bralcht and himself. He was not a natural meanderer and had to keep reminding himself that the faster he returned to the ward the longer he'd have to sit with Dan and think of something to say to him. And worse than that, he had to talk to Kelly, who was incapable of conversing in a sensible mutually inclusive manner, and Enschol Bralcht whose comments were few and guarded, but usually of an intensity that stopped conversations dead. Gavyn thought that there was something of death about everything Enschol Bralcht was involved in. The German, (Bog had informed Gavyn that Enschol Bralcht was German), when he was in the room, was both the centre of everything and the most forgettable thing. He was sort of like the death of a close friend: you forgot the details but the presence affected your every thought. Gavyn was happy to be away from the German and although not a natural meanderer, he was now wandering aimlessly through hospital corridors as if his meandering skills were inherited from a long line of meanderers of an Olympic standard.

It was a good twenty minutes before Gavyn returned to the ward with a cardboard tray holding three cups of steaming brown liquid. One of the liquids smelled heavily of coffee, one smelled of nothing but wet cardboard and one smelled of chicken soup — all three contained what the drinks machine claimed was tea. Gavyn was pleasantly surprised

67

when he returned. Enschol Bralcht was still staring at the corner of the room but Kelly's ability to talk about nothing-in-particular for hours at a time had found a good and heart-warming use as he was now telling Dan a story whilst the old man drifted in and out of consciousness. The story, as far as Gavyn could make out, having joined in halfway through its telling, was about a brave knight called Kelly who set out to fight an evil dragon for the hand of a beautiful maiden. Unfortunately, Kelly's mind was having difficulty following the plot and all the major characters were now named after himself and Kelly the dragon was in the process of rescuing the fire-breathing knight from evil Kelly; the princess who had eight arms and x-ray eyes. If you were semi-conscious, the story was a wonderful stream of images and words, but if you were awake enough to require sentences to fit together into sensible passages, you were in trouble.

What conclusion this story would have had, we can only guess at. Later in the car, Gavyn quizzed Kelly about this, but by that time Kelly had forgotten every detail of the tale. Gavyn tried to prompt him by asking if the knight's horse was going to marry the wizard, (both were called Kelly), and live happily ever after, but to no avail. The story would have reached its own strange ending were it not for the sudden BANG as the security camera in the corner of the ward exploded into black-plastic shrapnel; the sudden bang that caused Gavyn to throw steaming hot tea-like-liquid over himself, the sudden bang that proceeded the black smoke, that set off the fire alarms, that motivated the nurse to usher the visitors out of the ward.

On their way out, they passed a young man in a security guard outfit, with a toolkit clutched in his hands. The man was in a hurry and barely had time to offer Enschol Bralcht an evil glance. He obviously did not like him, but neither Kelly nor Gavyn understood why.

Back at the house, Bog and Michael sat in a circle of empty bottles that Michael had been carefully arranging to form some ancient sigil that he half-remembered was for good luck and protection against hangovers, (although he couldn't be entirely sure that he remembered that last bit correctly). Bog, with his higher capacity for alcohol was doing most of the talking now and Lynn had left her doorway vigil to return to neophyte Violet.

'You know what really irks me about Kelly?' said Bog.

'What?' slurred Michael.

'The way he can't seem to get my name right.'

'What?' said Michael again.

'Well my name is Bog, right?'

'Right.'

'And everyone calls me Bog, right?'

'Right.'

'So why does he persist in calling me Bob?'

'Not all the time,' said Michael, defending his absent guest.

'No, not all the time. One time, he called me Robert!'

Michael fell onto the floor from his sitting position and began laughing. He wasn't laughing about poor Kelly, nor was he laughing about his inability to balance, he was laughing at the word 'irk'. It was just such a great word. The more he thought about it, the more he laughed: 'Kelly's habits were irksome', 'Kelly was irkish', 'He possessed irkacity'. Bog laughed because Michael laughed, and laughter can be infectious, but the silly words in Michael's head remained hidden until the three hospital visitors returned half an hour later.

'What have we missed?'

Michael raised an arm, slowly and purposefully, as if it were immersed in treacle. He pointed at Kelly and moved his lips to say a word. 'Irk', he said, and fell over again laughing and Bog laughed too.

The three newcomers left the room with the sure knowledge that they were not going to get a sensible conversation from the kitchen tonight and it was probably time for bed.

Chapter Four
Always the Nice Ones

At the hospital, Jimmy, aping the doctors with whom he worked, was practicing surgery on the blackened remains of a camera. He was not happy. There was no reason for the fault. There was no obvious problem with miswiring or incorrect fuses or trapped gearing to cause over-heating. He was not a superstitious man. He prided himself on his logic, but somewhere in a locked-away corner of his mind, amongst the Sunday school naivety and his adolescent fascinations for TV programmes about ghosts and vampires, he suspected that the man in black had something to do with this. Jimmy hated that man for allowing doubt into his organised and comprehensive world-view. He replaced the camera with a brand new one. He took the dead machinery in his arms like a baby and returned to his station in the Portacabins. On the way, to cheer himself up, he fixed the drinks machine. It wasn't his responsibility, but he had

71

managed to get himself a reputation as someone who could fix anything and he enjoyed fixing the drinks machine. It wasn't that he was malicious, it was just that he was underpaid and over-educated, and the swapping of the supply tubes inside the machine was such a simple thing to do and the results made him happy. He spent many long hours in the security block, spying on people through his camera-eyes and watching them spit out the horrible liquids that they had just purchased in the belief that they were getting coffee. There is a reason why some people are employed in jobs involving talking to people, whilst some people, like Jimmy Chamberlain, were employed in a wooden shed next to the car park surrounded by computer and security monitors and far away from humanity.

The next day was Thursday and it was predictably a slow starting day. Michael came down to breakfast at the usual time, but instead of engaging the group with his usual positive thoughts for the day and what they would all achieve, he seemed to ignore the group and fumbled in some unbearably noisy kitchen drawers for a packet of pain-killers, swallowed them with a mouth full of orange juice and went back to bed, leaving the group leaderless and confused.

It was Bog, alcohol tolerant Bog, who eventually took the role of second-in-command. He began by explaining the night before's actions and conversations, to justify Michael's current condition. He then talked about the problem with finding a remote-enough place to practice 'primal-screaming' in Britain, and to illustrate the problem further, he brought Enschol Bralcht into the conversation.

' I bet you can scream as much as you like where you come from?'

'Oh yes,' said Enschol Bralcht in a disturbing monotone.' Where I have come from, people are always screaming.'

Despite this; the conversation continued, and Bog explained the plans that Michael and he had made for Thursday's entertainment. 'Today', he said, 'we shall be slowly introducing some ritual to you. Most of you will know bits and pieces of ritual already, but we really need to all be on the same wavelength so that on Friday we can be sure and safe for an exorcism. This is real magic folks! This is what we paid up for'.

This initiated a flurry of questions and comments. Some of the breakfasters thought that Bog's insinuation that they were novice ritualists was a little too patronising. Some others thought that this was an opportunity to force the program of events into new directions.

'What sort of ritual?'

'Can we perform some Celtic rituals?'

'Why are we so bound by Western traditions?'

'I've got a new athame that I'm dying to use.'

Enschol Bralcht remained silent. At the first mention of ritualistic magic however he made one of those odd facial expressions that was so similar to a smile, but wasn't quite right. Stranger still was Kelly's reaction to the hubbub. He too was silent. He had had something on his mind for the past 24 hours and appeared to be working out the best way to breach a particular subject. As the voices around him got louder and several debates about appropriate ritual became passionate and peppered with inappropriate language, his face showed some signs of decision and he opened his mouth. By reputation, a master of the non sequitur, when he finally spoke his incongruous remark ended all other debates. 'Um...' began Kelly, hesitantly, 'how long have you known Michael?'

'A couple of years, I guess', said Bog. 'Why?'

'Well... has he ever appeared to be a bit strange?' said Kelly.

Bog resisted the urge to quote the cliché about the pot calling the kettle black and instead allowed himself to be led by the curiously agitated Kelly to the garden and the shed at its far end.

Such was the mystery of the moment that the entire kitchen-load of pagans got up and followed Kelly, each person thinking what the secret might be, what Kelly might show them and what it would say about their hung-over and absent host.

Kelly opened the shed door with a flourish, like a stage magician or a man opening a coffin in a particularly corny zombie-movie. The action led the group to make a collective and involuntary gasp, which was followed by the collective and involuntary sense of guilt and stupidity as everyone peered into the shed and saw nothing particularly worth gasping about.

Kelly walked in, followed by the rest of the group, who were now mumbling amongst themselves in dissent. They stopped mumbling when Kelly pushed aside some papers and some boxes to show them the casket, which they duly stared at with questioning expressions on their faces, and when he opened the lid, (with a flourish that bore an even closer resemblance to those old zombie films), the silence of shock and disbelief that fell upon the crowd was palpable. One second. Two seconds. Three long seconds of silence allowed everyone time to go through the same mental gymnastics as Kelly had done and come to similar conclusions: Anyone who kept an Iron-Maiden torture device in his back shed was a strange fellow and possibly dangerous.

Bog's laughter, however, broke the silence and everyone turned to him for explanation,

'I know this story' he said with glee. 'I didn't know Michael then, but I know this story.' He began to rifle through the papers that were sitting in piles around his feet until he found a pack of photos. His audience was ready, but Bog continued to search for something, as the suspense built around him. He pulled out a photo and handed it to Lynn, who was immediately to his right, indicating that she should look at it and then hand it on to the next person. Then he started his story.

'A long time ago, there was a normal couple who lived in a normal house with a normal back garden with a normal old apple-tree in the corner. I don't know what order this next bit comes in, but either the man had a breakdown and left his normal job to try to better himself spiritually, which drove his wife away, or his wife left him and he then had a nervous breakdown which forced him to re-evaluate his life: body and soul. Whichever is the case, the unstable but highly motivated man read several books about holistically changing his life. One of the books was a Taoist text, which propagated the idea of calming the body as well as the spirit and the mind. He liked this idea, and although he didn't live on a mountain retreat in China he began building a box like those Taoist's had built, to try to train his body and mind to be still. The first thing he did was spend long periods in the box to force himself to get used to surviving without visual stimulus and freedom to move, to force his quiet mind and still body to remain quiet and still. Next, he hung the box from a branch of the tree. Although he couldn't see anything in there, his body and mind began to get used to the natural rhythm of the box, swaying in the wind and he began to tune himself to the patterns of nature.'

The photo had been passed round and was now returned to Bog. It showed a man and a woman standing next to each other with a garden behind them. The man looked a bit like Michael. The garden looked about as big as this garden, but the shed was smaller and instead of the paving and the pots of weeds that made the garden so individual, the garden in the photograph was a very ordinary suburban English garden with a large green lawn, carnations planted in the borders and a large old apple-tree as the focal point.

Bog continued: 'After stage two, Michael added the nails. The idea was that if he moved his body even slightly the nails would jab into him and remind him to keep still, stay conscious of the swaying but comfortable enough in the cramped surroundings to avoid fidgeting.' Bog paused.

To some members of the audience this practice seemed to make sense and Kelly, having studied Tai Chi in his youth, was already making up his mind to ask Michael if he could borrow the box.

'Michael was in the box, when the storm hit,' growled Bog. 'The idiot had either stopped watching the weather reports, or this was an unexpected squall. Whatever his excuse, when the branch broke and his box dropped with the windfall apples, he had to go to Addenbrookes and explain how he got his puncture wounds and when he came home he chopped down the tree and paved over the garden and vowed to leave the more extreme physical challenges alone and stick with mental training for a while.'

As the group filed out of the shed and back to the kitchen, they looked at the garden with its ornamental weeds with fresh eyes. The whimsy of a garden full of plants that most people would get rid of was still there, but now it was tempered with something else, something that had dwelt in this suburban atmosphere for so long that it was usually ignored: a dull feeling of disappointment, of plans that had never reached fruition and of dreams that would never bloom. Michael's life had changed dramatically over the last few years and his escape from the confinements of a conventional office job was a success that few people will ever know, but he still lived in a large house amongst other large houses owned by bankers and stockbrokers and the spirit of the suburbs.

Bog remained in the shed for a while and looked at a small piece of green paper that he found with Michael's other junk. It was a small part of a short story: not the beginning, nor the end. It didn't make any sense on its own, out of context, but that was the whole point. It was part of a project that Bog had been involved with ten years ago and if Michael was haunted by his past, it now seemed as if the hauntings were contagious. Bog, stood still, apparently stalwart and emotionless, but inside he was nauseous with nostalgia and melancholia.

'...wrapped in her blue robes. Thus it was Meredith who finally picked the panda up, polished the mud and gold dust off and put it in his substantive pockets. He grinned for both of them and uttering a short prayer got back onto his perambulator and rode back to Geneva, leaving the young drummer girl standing bathed in sunlight and gnosis.'

These were the words written on the strip of green paper and Bog could still remember which ones he had written and which ones his old friend Alan had written. Alan was now living somewhere in London, designing strange chaos magic web-sites and writing obscure graffiti across the capital's railway bridges and derelict buildings. Bog had lost touch with his old friend, but there was a slogan daubed in yellow spray paint on a bridge going into Kings Cross station that said 'Reality: Use it or Lose it' and he was sure that this was Alan's work.

Bog was the mechanic; blunt and practical. Alan was the artist; sharp and witty and unpredictable and for a while they had been an inseparable force for oddness in Cambridge. Cambridge however does not hold on to people like that for long. It's just another way station for London, which is the true siren for any weirdos who wish to make a career out of their weirdness.

Alan was the one who had given Bog his second Christening. When they first met, Bog was still using his legal name; Duncan O'Connell. As is traditional with friendships, this one grew to a stage when they were both comfortable with insulting each other and Alan, noting that Duncan's heritage was Irish, and his childhood had been spent trudging across his father's farmland, shooting rabbits, climbing trees and playing in ditches, began calling him 'Bog-Trotter' and later just 'Bog'. Bog, in return, called Alan all kinds of horrible names but few of them stuck. Alan was too fast and too mercurial for any nickname to take root.

One of Bog's insults that he reused with some frequency, though, was to call Alan a 'lunatic'. Alan had suffered from some sort of undefined psychosis before he had met Bog, and Bog was impressed that Alan was probably the only man he knew who could not only claim to be sane but had a piece of paper from a psychiatrist saying that he now was. However, Alan still suffered from headaches which were identified as symptoms of a much more serious condition. Every few years, he had to go to hospital where they would scan his head and if necessary put a tap in his skull to let an excess of fluid out. Bog reckoned that as the moon periodically grew closer to the planet, the tide inside Alan's body would rise and lead to headaches and some of his more interesting ideas, thus he was directly affected by the moon and was a true 'lunatic'. Bog's diagnosis had little founding in medical truth, but Alan thought it was funny and allowed himself to be called a 'Looney' by a man that he called 'Bog'.

Their first project together, instigated in an effort to introduce magic and wonder into people's lives, was an act of terrorism upon the restaurant industry of Cambridge. They would take it in turns to eat in different Chinese restaurants across the town, and when the opportunity presented itself they would switch the restaurant's own Fortune cookies for a batch that Alan and Bog had made. These were not poisonous or drugged in any literal sense of the word, but they might cause strange reactions, when unsuspecting customers read the messages that were contained within. The two terrorists had taken normal fortune cookies out of their wrappers, extracted the traditional bland fortunes, inserted their own messages and resealed the cookies. The innocuous 'you will receive good news from a relative' was replaced by the more paranoid 'your secret is no longer safe. Take drastic steps', and 'love will find a way' was now 'a small Welshman is planning insurrection. You are all that stands in his way.'

They went from attacks on Chinese restaurants to similar tricks with the mottos found in Christmas crackers, (Bog was particularly fond of 'Father Christmas does exist, but has been crucified upon a cross made from Norwegian Spruce. It is shedding blood and needles upon the carpet. Buy industrial stain-remover in the January Sales'). From there, the two began writing bits of stories on green paper and leaving them around town for people to pick up and puzzle over the meaning, and perhaps some people would find two or three of these pieces and try to put them together, with the understandable assumption that they would make one complete story. However, there was no complete story. Each piece of paper was a separate and incomplete paragraph. Alan reasoned that this was an analogy for our beliefs and religions, and we had to fight daily our own sophisms that told us that all the snippets of information that we had learned would eventually fit to form one universal truth. Alan believed that the universe was fractured.

Alan had left town ten years ago. Bog missed him but was a practical man, who had a number of friends still living in Cambridgeshire. He shook off the miasma of melancholia, placed his thoughts back into the shed inside his head, where he kept his discarded past amongst the motorcycle parts, and rejoined his friends.

Chapter Five
Intolerance

The talks and demonstrations of magic would begin in the afternoon. There was still far too much to do this morning. Gavyn and Violet were sent into town with the film, which held the group's portrait. They were instructed to go to a 24 hour developing shop, so that the group could get the results back on Friday: the last full day that they would be together. Lynn volunteered to coax Michael out of bed, fill him with vitamin C and place him in his beautiful but melancholic garden to breathe in the air and return to a more useful state. Meanwhile Bog, Enschol Bralcht and Strange Kelly were left with the worst chore. Bog, remembering that there were environmental influences to any exorcism, reasoned that to free Michael of his ex-wife's spirit, the clutter of the kitchen (a symbol of his failure to accept his singularity and tidy the room himself) must be tidied. As Gavyn would have attested, were he not stuck in a traffic jam in a big squinting car, this was crazy-logic. No-one should have to clean the kitchen. It should just be condemned or perhaps napalmed and the ground salted in a ritual manner to insure that the foul thing did not grow back again. But Bog had persuaded himself that it needed doing and his reasoning, crazy as it was, was powerful enough to persuade Enschol Bralcht and Kelly to help.

The first thing that they needed to do was to find some cleaning products. For a while Bog thought he might have to use some paper towels and some of the plum wine to clean the entire room (it seemed to have dissolved a trail in the scum in the sink since Michael had poured some away last night). Luckily though Enschol Bralcht managed to find some bleach and surface cleaner in the cupboard under the sink. However, typical of the foreigner, he had been sitting on the floor examining the bottles for some time before Kelly confirmed that they were useful. Enschol Bralcht seemed at times to have very little knowledge of English and despite the pictures of sparkling kitchens advertised on the packaging, his mind did not seem to equate this with the task at hand. Perhaps he was just distracted. Perhaps his mind was elsewhere. Maybe he was too busy thinking about the forthcoming magical ritual. Bog had noticed him smiling, out of the corner of his eye, when he announced what they would be doing this afternoon.

The actual work, however, managed to wipe the smile off Enschol Bralcht's face. The three worked hard and well together: Bog orchestrating (and doing the bits he didn't trust the others to do), Kelly, determined but easily distracted, flittering about the kitchen in a flurry of action like a hummingbird with a dishcloth, and Enschol Bralcht cleaning the most disgusting areas without even flinching. Enschol Bralcht was a real boon to the others, because although he was neither as quick as Kelly nor as organised as Bog, he could extract the rotting things from the sink without throwing up. He had an ability to seem almost oblivious to his surroundings. Kelly believed that this might be due to some sort of internal meditation and was very impressed. Bog suspected that it might be due to some sort of lack of understanding. Enschol Bralcht, however, kept working: he did not seem to need a rest, he did not complain, he was the most focussed of the cleaners and yet Kelly and Bog had the strange feeling that at times he wasn't even really there.

They spent two hours cleaning the kitchen, and even then they didn't touch the oven or the top shelves. They limited themselves to the surfaces and the floor and the bin and the sink. They stowed away all the brown paper bags full of shopping and threw away two sacks of sell-by-date pensioners. And whilst all this was being accomplished, upon one of the new shiny clean surfaces Bog was putting aside a catalogue of items that he thought might be useful: a large Tupperware container with sealable lid, a carton of sea-salt, clove oil, basil, cumin, lilac, mint and rosemary.

When Gavyn and Violet returned with a receipt for a film and a stack of Vegan Pizzas (Bog had insisted that no-one was going to mess up his kitchen by cooking in it... at least, not yet!) the seven pagans sat down at the shiny kitchen table and devoured the fare, whilst making favourable comments on the cleanliness of the surroundings. None of them had the nerve to ask if they could go elsewhere to eat the Pizza, despite everyone's eyes watering from the bleach fumes that were swirling in an almost perceptible mist around them.

The group were democratic or perhaps anarchic or communist because when it came to organising who should do what for the afternoon's ritual, there was no arguing: everyone assumed a role akin to their own nature and experience. Thus it was decided that a ritual space would be created, separate (at least in the psyche of the group) from the mundane space and it would be a circle marked at its cardinal points by people representing the elemental forces of nature. The reason for this was that no matter what books the individuals had read a similar 'casting of circle' ritual appeared in most of their 'traditions'. Only Violet, steeped in the belief that oriental religions held the true path, suspected that the 'traditions' seldom went back further than the Victorian revival and were less universal than Lynn, for instance, passionately believed. Violet could not see how a system so entrenched in its invocation of the four Hellenistic elements could be so dogmatically followed, whilst her

Chinese and Indian books told her that there were five elements and not four. Why could they not invoke the five Chinese elements? And if the number of elements was arbitrary and if it was true that Science and Art should meet in magic, why not use the one hundred and twelve elements of the periodic table? She knew the answer before she opened her mouth to question the group: the chance of getting a coven, moot or group of one hundred and twelve pagans together in a cooperative manner was slim, if not wholly impossible. But still, she loved the image that played in her mind of various people, dressed in robes, standing forth and uttering lines such as 'I invoke Mercury: quick-silver, the anachronistic liquid metal, a winged god of poison' or more obscurely 'I invoke Technetium, the stellar spirit, heavy and radioactive to the tune of 200 counts per minute', instead what Violet got was the following:

Everyone helped clear the front-room's floor of the cigarette packets, cushions and empty bottles that had magically accumulated since Wednesday's Tai Chi. Then Bog took a needle from his wallet and running it along the blade of a vicious looking pen-knife he magnetized it and located North for Michael (Michael having lived in the house for a dozen years practicing all kinds of magical rituals already knew which way was North, but did not want to interrupt Bog's part in the ritual. Bog liked playing with knives and to stop him might put him in a bad mood that could affect the whole room's atmosphere). Michael then placed a small wooden box in the centre of the room and extending a wooden stick, (actually a piece of thorn that Michael had sacrilegiously broken off a rather sacred thorn bush in Glastonbury), Michael pointed towards the North. He walked to the furthest Northern point of an imaginary circle and then walked the imaginary circle's circumference clockwise, marking it with a non-existent white light that shot from a wand that was a thorn twig in the reality that was not Michael's reality. 'The circle is perfect,' he said to himself. And it was. He walked around it a second time saying, 'I cast this circle to protect us from the energies that might do us harm. I draw into the circle only the energies that are right for us at this time and in this place.' Then he walked around it a third time and announced that it was done.

Now it was time for the invocations. Bog moved to the Eastern cardinal point of the circle, and spoke a mixture of his own beliefs and those expected of him:

'Hail Guardians of the Watchtower of the East: the air spirits, sylphs and siroccos. We welcome you and your protection.'

Meanwhile Violet was letting her imagination run wild and was thinking, 'Hail to the Watchtower of 90 degrees, the Spirit of Oxygen, Euphoria in excess, sustainer of all animal life and aerobic reactions. '

Then Kelly, standing at the Southernmost point of the circle spoke: 'Hear me, spirits of flame and fire. I call upon you at the watchtower of the South to aid us in our rites'. He then carved a quick symbol with his index finger in the air, as if his finger was a sparkler on bonfire night.

'Hail to Magnesium,' thought Violet, 'brought into fiery life when combined with oxygen. Hail the spirits whose number is twelve. Hail the dancing deities of flash photography.'

Then Lynn to the West said, 'Hail Guardians of the Watchtower of the West. I do summon you to witness our rite and guard this circle. Powers of Water, give us thy cleansing essence as we journey between the worlds. We welcome you.'

And Violet, enjoying herself, echoed inside her head 'Hail the Hydrogen Watchtower. Hail to spirits whose atomic number is one. Hail the most universal and hail the most abundant.'

Finally, (and predictably), Michael, now at the Northern point of his invisible circle, said 'Hail Xenophanes, Guardians of the Watchtower of the North. I summon you to witness our rite and guard this circle. Powers of Earth, bring us thy nourishing and grounding essence. We come from earth and from earth we will return.'

'Hail Carbon, the organic element, without which there would be no flesh or blood, hail Graphite and Diamond and Buckminsterfullerine: the physical made mundane, rare and peculiar. Hail the power of the earth: the fossil fuel gods that gave man his first push towards cultural evolution.'

Michael, ignorant of the Violet variations, then walked to the central point where he had placed a wooden chest as a makeshift altar. He opened the lid and pulled out a large shallow bowl, a Tupperware tub full of water, some paper and pens and the collection of flavourings and additives that Bog had extracted from the kitchen. He sprinkled a little sea-salt, clove oil, basil, cumin, lilac, mint and rosemary in the shallow bowl and added some frankincense from a small vial in his pocket. Then he stirred the water to make a bowl of nice smelling but fairly horrible-looking oily thin soup. He then handed out pieces of the paper, (the same paper that he had used at Grantchester), to each member of the group, who were now standing solemnly within their sacred space. He told them to write on their paper something that they wanted to be rid of and then make a paper boat and place it in the water. Bog knew who was the crew for Michael's boat (a wife who should have sailed out of his life some years ago but whose memory still clung to him) but nobody knew what anyone else had written. They then waited an interminably long time for the boats to absorb the water and sink. Apparently, the flowing water of the Cam was much better at sinking ships than Michael's stagnant sweet pool. They stood in silence for fifteen minutes before they judged the armada was sufficiently scuppered and Michael led the thanking of the guardians of the watchtowers and the anti-clockwise sweeping away of the sacred circle.

The fifteen minutes of silence slowly gave way to

small-talk as Gavyn fetched out some celebratory wine from the kitchen and Bog disposed of the water, (herbs, boats and all), back into the Tupperware container and placed the lid firmly on top. This would be disposed of in the Cam on the way to see Dan, later in the evening. Any food or drink left from a post-ceremonial snack was also destined to be ritually buried beneath the stinging nettles but there was little chance of any alcohol being left by this crowd.

This evening it had been decided that Bog, Lynn and Violet should go to Addenbrookes and Michael, Gavyn, Kelly and Enschol Bralcht should stay at the house and work out what to do for the ritual-proper: tomorrow's grand exorcism. This fact-finding mission started in an earnest fashion with Michael taking Gavyn, Kelly and Enschol to his bedroom to sort out a few books for research purposes.

Michael's room was similar to everyone else's except whilst the guest rooms were kept sparse and airy and tidy, his room was different. In horror movies, there is a clichéd trap called the 'shrinking room', where a character (usually a young lady with a penchant for ear-splitting screaming) enters a room, only to discover the door has locked behind her and through some elaborate and unlikely machinery, the walls start to move together, breaking up the furniture as they move. The main character panics and fumbles at the door handle but the cinema audience know that it is in vain, the walls will clamp together and then the screams will stop.

Michael's room looked a little like this scene, or

perhaps a little like this scene if it had been played out in the British library. The room seemed too small for the books it contained. They spilled out from under his bed. They formed dangerous Tower of Pisa-like stacks up the walls. They sat in piles upon the windowsill, which meant that only thin beams of light could nudge past them to enter the room and illuminate the dust that danced in the air like a shaken-up snow-globe. The only sensible conclusion was that this was once a much larger, tidier and better-organised library and as the room shrank its contents were beginning to buckle and bulge and break. This wasn't far from the truth. When Michael had hit upon the idea of opening his house to paying guests, he'd had the difficult job of clearing their rooms to make habitable guest accommodation. Some of the bits and pieces had ended up in the new shed. The books and occult reference material had all been brought into Michael's room, and the attic had taken the rest of the strain.

Kelly was delighted and sat down in the middle of the floor, (in the middle of a pile of books), with a grin on his face like a small child surrounded by new toys. Gavyn looked a little less pleased. He had managed to avoid tidying the dreaded kitchen and was worried that this room might be Bog's next unwise project. Enschol Bralcht looked nonchalant or aloof, but when Michael looked at him for a reaction he tried one of his smiles. He was getting better, but Michael was beginning to suspect that Mr. Bralcht had been lying to him. His grave and unimposing manner, the confusion when presented with Western cleaning products and his unpractised smile: all suggested that he was from Eastern Europe — Poland perhaps.

'Surely you don't need all these books?'

'Of course I do, Gavyn,' said Michael without a pause for thought, 'Something's got to keep the bedside cabinet up.' And he pointed to a sorry-looking piece of furniture which as well as supporting a small stack of his most recently acquired reading material, was itself resting on three good wooden legs and one stack of books: a surrogate limb for a missing appendage.

'You know, you could use one of our rooms, to store some of your books,' said Gavyn. Gavyn and Violet, although a couple, were treated equally to others and had one room each in the house. Currently, they used one as a bedroom, where they shared a single bed, with limbs overflowing like a beached octopus, and one room was used as a dressing-room/wash-room.

'That's OK,' said Michael. 'I like it like this. I have this theory that whilst I'm sleeping the high volume of learning represented in this room leaches from the crowded pages and into my open mind. I'm learning by osmosis. Perhaps if my mind were more open, I'd never have to read a book again.'

'Your kidding, right?' said Gavyn, unsure.

'Mostly,' said Michael with a smile, running his hand

along a stack of books that leaned over his bed like a welcoming tree bower, from the lowest trunk of Norse and Egyptian mythology, through the commentaries on Tarot, through Roman history, Greek symbology, Children's literature, the Ramayana, and much to Gavyn's secret delight, the Bible.

In a coldly-decorated ward, somewhere in the small city of University buildings, research centres, and medical practices that calls itself Addenbrookes lay Old Dan, in a state of impressive delusion. In his youth, when not actually working towards his post-graduate degree, he had worked towards keeping his body and soul intact, which in expensive Middle-Class Cambridge was a difficult matter. Old Dan's solution, made possible by his rower's physique, had been to give tours of the City from the back of a punt. He had been paid generously by tourists as he showed them Christopher Wren's architecture and Newton's Engineering from the waterborne vantage point. Thus he was able feed himself again, for another week, and stay in Cambridge all year and never have to go back to his parents with open hands and an open wallet. Cambridge punts are a remarkable way to see a remarkable city, as Old Dan, himself, used to remark. They are a remnant of the era when the fens reached as far as the City and flat-bottomed boats were the only logical way of getting around the reed-infested waterways that provided so much of the trade and industry of the region. But for some reason the long coffin-shaped boats remained even when the fens were pushed back and the river de-reeded. Any logical boat-builder would now supply the city with more stable boats with deeper keels. And that same boat-builder would recommend oars that, although prone to tangle in any remaining water-plants, would provide a more sensible and steerable propulsion system than the big stick that the standing punter had to use to push himself along. But Cambridge is an old City and averse to sudden changes: the punts remain, and although you can hire one and propel it yourself, (colliding into banks, water-fowl and other punts as you go), it is often safer to allow an energetic young student to do it for you.

When young Dan, became old Dan, he found it more and more difficult to hold onto a job that necessitated youthful vigour and he moved on to the next logical step for a man in love with a City. He took his local knowledge and packed away his straw boater and came onto dry land to drive the open-top tourist buses around the City. Over a radio mike he told the swarms of bloated Americans and chattering Japanese and the Italians, and the French and every passenger of every nation about the weird and wonderful history of the City that he had come to when he was eighteen and had never left.

This is all an explanation for the condition of Old Dan, when Lynn, Bog and Violet entered the ward: there were many delusional patients in there mumbling about their loved ones, but only one man was giving a tour of Cambridge through time and space as he lay amongst the cotton sheets and the warm drugs.

In answer to Violet's jovial, 'How's Addenbrookes treating you?', came the answer, 'Addenbrookes? John Addenbrooke was a doctor who was less than content with damp Cambridge's reputation as the best place to get the plague outside of London. On his deathbed in 1719, he left the City a good deal of money and asked that it be used to build a hospital. The Cambridge councillors and elders leapt upon this idea with the speed that one has learnt to expect from Cambridge, and forty-seven years later the building work began...'

Dan's commentary was cut short by the appearance of a priest asking if he could help in any way. Perhaps it was the interruption that Lynn found rude or perhaps it was just that since she had found her calling and built her belief system, she had seen the dog-collar as a symbol of hatred. Whatever it was in the poor priest's manner that upset Lynn, the results were explosive.

'How dare you come here bothering sick people with your talk of God! Don't you know that this man is a pagan? He doesn't need you. He doesn't want you and we don't want you here'.

The priest was visibly shocked by this. He was an amiable man and an experienced 'hospital visitor' and quite used to the strength of feelings that some people held when God tests their friends and relatives in the apparently cruel way that he tested Job before them, but this attack seemed unprovoked. He had, after all, only come into the ward, (avoiding walking under the ladder where a maintenance man fixed a security camera because even men of God afford themselves a few superstitions), to tell Dan's visitors how much he admired Dan. In his role of 'comforter to the sick and delusional' he had already had a number of bizarrely one-way conversations with the old patient; during which the priest would bring up a topic and Dan would deliver a glassy-eyed but apparently lucid monologue about how the subject fitted into the history of Cambridge.

Upon entering the ward at lunchtime and asking how 'the little something the cooks had prepared' was, he was impressed by Dan's ramblings in Latin and old English about 'Parva Cokeria'; the little cooking, or 'Petty Cury'. The same phrase was used as a street name, where presumably the chefs of Cambridge used to live and across from which lay the Falcon Inn, as visited by Samuel Pepys and allegedly Queen Elizabeth I, when she was in need of a reception hall in the City. Then later in the 1950's, 60's and 70's it was home to the Cambridge Footlights: those applauded young comedians who had reached their heyday with Jonathan Miller and Peter Cook and Monty Python and Douglas Adams. Then, later still, in that smoky dive and in an age of breaking taboos, Sylvia Plath's eyes had fallen upon a young

Ted Hughes and poetry was born. Now the Falcon has been flattened and its name obliterated by its rival The Lion Inn; as the Lion Yard shopping centre sits heavily upon these foundations.

The nurses did not share the priest's delight at Dan's condition, however. They despaired that their patient might ever talk 'normally' again. They didn't know his background though, or about his love affair with Cambridge, and that Dan's normality like most of his fellow pagans was adjacent but never fully synchronised with other people's normality.

The priest apologised for causing offence, (although a little unsure how he had achieved this), and red-faced in embarrassment left the ward, not noticing that he had backed out underneath the portentous ladder.

Lynn glowed, flushed with success at having driven away her perceived demon, while Violet and Bog blushed in sympathy with the priest and a little in anger at their passionate but unkind companion. Never had the magnolia-coloured ward room filled with so much bright colour.

Dan, meanwhile, oblivious to most of his surroundings, had picked up on Lynn's battle for his soul as an excuse to talk about religion. '...this city was built on religion,' he argued to no one in particular. 'In the 13th century, a truly international body of scholars called Dominicans and Franciscans were linking Europe up with their shared language and their shared curiosity for understanding how God's universe worked. They set up

98

colleges and filled them with young priests and exiles from the riots in Oxford ('the other-place'). The Bishop of Ely was the main backer at this stage, but there were other religious forces in action in the fens. Most of the trade at the time involved another international body, the Jews. These men of the elder faith were ghettoised even then and held close ties with enclaves across the known world, through which they traded goods eventually to the gentiles. To deny the Ibrahemic religions is to deny Cambridge its origins and its special beauty: from Christchurch to Magdalene to St. John's, religion is in the architecture and the nomenclature and the streets and the blood of the city...' And so he went on. His voice was a low soporific drone like the background sound of the air-conditioning: something you only notice when you listen out for it, or when every other sound is silenced.

Perhaps the pagan group would have paid more attention to Dan, who was, after all, their purpose for being there, but having dismissed the priest they had inadvertently set off a chain reaction in the ward and somewhere up a ladder by the doorway, someone was seething.

Jimmy Chamberlain, fixing the security camera, witnessed the whole thing from his elevated vantage point. Although a militant non-believer, he had a compartmentalist mind that said that some believers were worse than others. His opinion of the priest was low: here was a man who had dedicated his life to a delusional belief in a single personality for the entire universe and a saviour that clearly did not save us from any of life's hardships. He had an even lower opinion, though, of people who made up their own beliefs from apparently little empirical evidence but were so stoic in their convictions that they were prepared to insult anyone who possessed a different sophism.

'You didn't have to be so rude!' he bellowed from the top step of the ladder: his voice raining down upon the surprised pagans like an artillery barrage. It took them a while to realise where the voice had come from and this allowed Jimmy to press his advantage. He slowly made his way down the ladder, with eyes fixed on Lynn, issuing forth proclamations like a secular preacher.

'You didn't have to do that. He didn't mean any harm. He's cared for the patient far more than any of you have,' he said, giving away his voyeuristic tendencies. There was little that went on in the hospital that he hadn't seen through his cameras and even if the one in this ward was faulty he knew who had entered the room and when.

They were stunned. Lynn's outburst had been uncalled-for but this reciprocal outburst seemed even less warranted. Violet thought that 'stunned' was not quite the right word and was surprised to find that for the first time in her life she had found a use for the most unlikeliest of words: flabbergast. Here in a whispering ward room a loud argument was about to erupt with them in the centre of it, with little warning of it's coming and no way of stopping it.

'How do you know what we've been doing for Dan?' shouted Lynn.

Shhhh,' hissed Bog, waving his arms in a quieting gesture, fully aware of the acceptable volume for a hospital ward.

'We've been praying, and visualising and casting spells since this first happened,' Lynn continued and Violet's and Bog's hearts sank to their shoes. No matter how much they shared Lynn's beliefs, they were fully aware of how silly her statement sounded and how, by association, silly they must also seem. They felt embarrassed and also guilty that perhaps their convictions weren't as strong as Lynn's.

'Oh, I'm sure he feels much better now,' said Jimmy with all the spite he could muster. Then he spotted the piece of quartz or whatever semi-precious piece of rock was hanging around Lynn's neck and he smiled an unseen smile and launched a new tirade:

'And look at you with your stones around your neck and wrists and fingers, because you are believers in natural healing and have no faith in medicine and yet you come into medicine's shiny cathedral without an ounce of guilt for your blasphemies, and what is the symbol of your support for Mother Nature?... a lump of quartz that may or may not vibrate at a suitable frequency to aid your heart chakra or some-such twaddle. Have you ever been to Brazil and seen

101

the environmental damage caused by your narrow-minded beliefs? Have you seen the origins of your symbolic piece of nature, ripped from the ground in open pit quarries that shatter the surrounding tranquillity, poison the water and leave a haemorrhaging scar in the wilderness? And the need for semi-precious stones is growing to feed the Western hunger for physical ownership of the planet, but this time it's not called colonialism, imperialism or greed, it's called crystology, crystography, crystal-healing, witchery, paganism and even nature-loving. You make me sick!'

And then, his eloquent outburst was ruined by his less-than eloquent visual punctuation. He picked up his ladder and folded it under his arm, gestured to them in a non-magical way and said 'Read my aura!' and left.

The sudden drop in the volume of conversation was dramatic. Even Lynn had nothing to say and the room's normal low noises rose back to prominence: the occasional coughing, the whir of the air conditioning and Old Dan having a conversation with himself about magical auras and Doctors John Dee and Simon Forman, who both brought magic and charlatanry to sixteenth century Cambridge, and who both had bad endings, and lots of other useless facts in which no one was currently interested.

The other patients began to pretend that they hadn't heard the fracas and returned to their sleeping, coughing and grumbling. Junior doctors and nurses put their heads around the door to check what the disturbance was and finding that they had missed it, returned to their rounds. Violet, Lynn and Bog turned to face Dan, searching for something to say, whilst still smarting from verbal injuries.

Violet, who had an elderly aunt, was not unfamiliar with these situations and began to tell Dan about the pagan retreat in Cherry Hinton and what they had all been up to during the week, until Lynn, with only the occasional aside at how rude the security officers were, joined in the report. Telling delirious patients the news was the accepted thing to do, but it was unlikely that it was really being listened to. Dan was still completing his mumbling monologue about the dodgy Doctor Simon Forman and his decidedly un-magical ways of ensuring successful pregnancies in the wives of his patients. Only Bog was silent.

Chapter Six
The Curious Calm of the Readers

Bog was no longer a member of a motorcycle gang, because he had mellowed with age and because he no longer had a bike, but he still found it difficult to accept criticism without distributing an act of violence in return, or at the very least a menacing look. Lynn's anger was now dying to the level of a disagreement and Violet had an air of calmness and control that she shared with Gavyn, but Bog felt like he had been attacked and felt like he needed retribution. He was not a verbose man, and the little he knew of the security officer told him that he could not win an argument with him, and so for five minutes whilst everyone else talked and no-one listened, he schemed.

Violet and Lynn were talking about Wednesday, whilst Dan was in the nineteenth century, talking about Trinity College where Aleister Crowley was trying to be a poet and a mountaineer, and any idea that he was a magician was yet to come. Then Bog spoke. Interrupting the day and the year, he asked them to wait for him. He said he'd be gone for a couple of hours and that he had something important to do. Violet and Lynn were naturally curious but Bog was not going to give away his plan until nearer its completion. It would be bad luck, and luck and magic were linked like the twin serpents that were illustrated throughout the hospital as a medical crest (the symbol of Hermes, god of communication, thieves and for some: magic).

Bog left the ward with a purposeful stride. He spat upon his index finger and undoing a shirt button, he pushed his hand through to his chest and drew upon it in saliva, a sigil: 'a charm of charm', as he called it. He did not know where he had first come across it or even if he had invented it himself, but for years he had performed this little gesture whenever he needed to talk the birds out of the trees or the hind legs off a donkey.

The charm of charm was one part nine-pointed star and one part coiled snake and he used it (perhaps even needed to use it) before job interviews, first dates and infrequent meetings with police officers. Some people believe in magic. Some people prove its existence by showing sceptics examples of how odd things are caused to occur by odd means. Sceptics still insist that these are just coincidences.

The fact that the radiologist was a biker was a

coincidence: the sort of coincidence that occurred now and then to Bog when he needed it. Bog and the radiologist talked for half an hour about their shared two-wheeled passion and then the radiologist went against all wisdom and several major hospital regulations and took Bog into the MRI room.

MRI (or Magnetic Resonance Imaging) was the latest toy of the Radiology field, and as Bog remembered reading in the newspaper, Addenbrookes Radiology Department had one of the newest of the new toys. The newspaper had suggested that what made this MRI unit special and the pride of East Anglia was that the magnetic pulse was less powerful and the computer analysis software cleverer, which meant that, in theory, it might be useable by patients with cardiac monitors, pace-makers and metal splints for bones and joints. Previously, these people had been prohibited from this equipment, as the magnetic field that shifts the hydrogen atoms to allow a computer to make up a three dimensional map of the body would also have strange effects on metal splints and potentially deadly effects on pace-makers.

The radiologist acknowledged that most of what Bog had read was true and asked him to remove any metallic objects before entering the scan room. Bog didn't think he was a ferric-fetishist but by the time he'd removed his earrings, rings, bracelet, wristwatch, belt (with metal buckle), boots (metal buckle), jeans (metal zips and rivets) and jacket (metal buttons and zips) he was practically naked. Then Bog was asked a number of questions about the metal pins in his leg: how long they had been there and how much trouble they had been since they were put in. Bog answered jovially and truthfully, whilst all the time maintaining that a curiosity about the inside of his leg was the only reason that he wished to go through with this.

The radiologist then told Bog what to expect. They were going to place him on a trolley, with a type of temporary caste about his leg and then he would go feet first into a loud thudding electromagnetic tunnel. The noise and claustrophobia would be intense and the radiologist gave Bog a pair of headphones linked to a CD player in the computer room and it was agreed (with much nostalgia) that 'The Best of Hawkwind' would be ideal music with which to relax the patient. The radiologist also admitted that even with the patient's own choice of music, sometimes the nausea of being placed in a large noisy magnetic coil is too much to bear, and one reason for the recent upgrade of machinery that the paper failed to report was that the old machine was starting to smell of vomit. Bog was happy to test the new machine.

For thirty minutes he lay inside the magnet; dreaming of revenge and anxious that his time was running out. He had agreed to meet Violet and Lynn in the car park in two hours time and unnaturally watch-less he wasn't sure whether he had spent one hundred and twenty minutes away from them or perhaps just sixty. He ended up measuring time by

Hawkwind tracks. Understanding that most were 4 minutes long, the six songs he'd listened to meant that he'd been in the tube for approximately twenty four minutes. Some of Hawkwind was improved by the addition of a deep bass drum and some became an annoying mess of sound as the two out-of-sync beats collided and separated in turn.

When the procedure was finally over and the radiologist came back into the scan room to disconnect all the bits that needed to be disconnected, Bog sat up to face a hang-over from a drink he had never drunk. He staggered as he dressed, and although for the purpose of pretence he was supposed to be interested in his results, he told his co-conspirator that he had to go and meet an urgent appointment, apologised and left through the back door.

The reason for the back door exit was not embarrassment or secrecy about his unwarranted medical procedure. It was simply to avoid passing too many metal objects and equipment sensitive to magnetic fields. As soon as Bog was out in the open air he had the urge to test the after-effects of his treatment and so, pulling a fluff-covered paperclip from his pocket and rolling up his trouser-leg, he was delighted to see the paperclip stick to his skin, as did his keys and his watch and the tags on the end of the zips on his leather jacket pointed towards his calf like compass needles.

As he walked back to the car park, (a long journey made longer by nausea and the confusing scale and layout of the Addenbrookes site), he realised that his little test was unnecessary: his surroundings provided all the test data an amateur scientist could wish for. Every metal lamppost seemed to attract him as if he was a beagle with a full-bladder, and for a car-phobic individual he was possessed by a need to see every vehicle at a closer glance.

Meanwhile, in a wooden Portacabin, amongst the banks of surveillance monitors, Jimmy Chamberlain was still in a state of agitation. He felt he had won the verbal battle with the New Age nutters, but he found no peace in victory. The atheistic argument had been raging in his head for years, and a five-minute rant had not been enough to release the pressure within him. It just reminded him that it was there.

A few years ago, the already sceptical Jimmy Chamberlain had been living with a girl who believed in 'all that stuff', and in the spirit of love and compromise he accompanied her to a spiritual healing road-show at a conference centre just outside the city. There he found hell. There was no debating, no questioning and seemingly no intelligence under the conference centre's cavernous roof. There were people behind tables, along four aisles, and each table gave Tarot readings, sold healing crystals, promoted acupuncture, sold incense, demonstrated Reiki, sold handcrafted sticks (blessed as wands), sold metal bowls (cauldrons), sold bad Batik (ceremonial altar cloths), and sold and sold and sold.

On the other side of the tables were streams of the gullible middle-class, each rebelling against his or her boring mundane life by believing in anything (absolutely anything) that seemed more interesting. Their minds and mouths and purses were open and Jimmy Chamberlain felt like the last living human at the closing stages of a zombie movie.

However, just because these were the undead it didn't mean that they were a uniform bunch, such as the drab undead commuters that groan and stagger their way to London every day, or the grey undead politicians who clutter up the television screens ineffectually fighting for their piece of the graveyard. The mindless corpses that surrounded Jimmy were a delight to the visual cortex: there were rainbow coloured ponchos that should have been destroyed in the Sixties, there were a variety of camouflaged combat trousers dyed in vivid colours, as if the wearers were prepared to fight wars on Mars or Venus, (and some of them probably were), and there was hair in braids, in ribbons, and in unkempt matted dreadlocks.

Jimmy's favourite zombie was a middle aged woman with a large ginger 'afro' haircut that might have been fashionable in the Seventies. Amongst the wonders on display at the road show, there was a man with a Kirlian camera taking pictures of a whole queue of people eager to see their auras. The Kirlian camera works on the principle of exposing the photographic plate to a high-voltage electrical field. There is one school of thought that says that the life-force of a creature interferes with the electrical field and the coloured halo produced on the photograph is a representation of this aura. There is another school of thought that says that the electrical grounding, humidity and temperature of the subject affects the photograph and no auras are involved. To be fair, the emotional state of people having their photograph taken will affect their temperature and humidity and thus Kirlian technology can act as a two-dimensional mood-ring, but the halos that commonly surround a subject's head say far more about perspiration than parapsychology.

The ginger-afroed woman was in the queue for her Kirlian portrait. She got to the front and, with a big smile on her face, attached the electrodes to her fingers and faced the camera. The man said 'smile' even though she already was. When cameramen say 'smile' it means something else: it's code for 'I'm pressing the button now whether you like it or not'. If the woman had a big smile when the photograph was taken, then her smile at the end of the session when her photograph was developed was immense. The photographer showed her the picture, took her money and explained what the various colours on the picture meant in connection with her psyche. Jimmy was intrigued and looked over her shoulder and almost burst out laughing. The woman's out of focus photograph did indeed present her with a large orangey halo around her head: like the orange/gold aura that you would expect to find around a psychic healer personality or indeed a woman with a big orange afro!

Bog believed in auras. He saw no reason to doubt that

science did not yet have all the answers and he hated people who dismissed those with ideas beyond the narrow confines of the text-books, as mad or misguided. If electrical fields (and magnetic fields) can extend beyond a body then why couldn't other energies; including whatever energies make up that indefinable essence of life? He remembered a conversation, or at least a part of a conversation that he'd had with Enschol Bralcht, when he had been told with unshakeable resolve that 'all energy is life' and that 'all matter is energy.' This didn't in itself mean anything, but the intensity with which Enschol Bralcht imbued these phrases meant that they stuck in your mind for far longer than the rest of the conversation, or indeed what Enschol Bralcht sounded like or looked like. There was something insubstantial about poor Enschol Bralcht.

Bog's reminiscences were halted suddenly by an epiphany. He was rapidly passed by an ambulance with its blue lights flashing and he suddenly understood what his radiologist had been talking about. Their conversation had been a mixture of practical advice (mostly about MRI) and small talk (mostly about bikes), but other things had crept into the conversation, including Ecnalubma which sounded Welsh but Bog assumed these were some sort of pieces of medical equipment. At the time, Bog did not question the radiologist. He was in a hurry to get the procedure over with and he liked the man too much to interrupt the conversation with dumb questions. The charm of charm worked that way: everyone liked you and you liked everyone. It was a bit like taking a symbolic version of ecstasy without the risk of terminal dehydration.

Now a second ambulance raced past Bog and he smiled as he briefly saw the letters on the front of it: reversed so that you could read it clearly in a car's rear-view mirror. It said ecnalubma. It was surprising that the ecnalubma didn't stop and throw Bog in the back. His erratic walking from lamp post to metal railing and back to lamp post, made him look like one of the patients from the head injuries ward, or at the very least a drunk, in need of drying-out. But Bog continued his walk: his persistence fuelled by the lack of remaining time he had left to exact his revenge on the security officer.

When he finally rounded the outpatients' building and gazed across the car park he was relieved to see that Violet and Lynn were not yet standing there, waiting for him. He still had time. He made his way with his electromagnetic limb to the car park where he had agreed to meet up with his colleagues and though the sky was a perfect British battleship grey, as he leant back upon the Portacabin he smiled up at the firmament and what little heat there was in the air was absorbed by his face. He was a happy little man in the depths of his happy little revenge.

Of course assumptions had been made; but as these proved correct Bog did not feel that he had relied too much on Lady Luck. Instead, he felt a mixture of smugness and a comfort that he was part of the great thing; the fate, the God, the whatever. This was one of those times that enough of the cogs had been revealed for you to believe in the machinery of the universe. Bog had seen signs to the temporary location of the Security Office when he had first entered the hospital, hours earlier. He had remembered the newspaper article about MRI at Addenbrookes and Bog needed revenge against a security officer, who cradled security cameras in his arms like newborn babies.

Behind Bog there were muffled shouts and curses. Portacabin walls are not that thick: they cannot hold back a scream nor, it seems, a strong electromagnetic current, and inside Jimmy was rattling keyboards with the frantic frustration of a man forsaken by his microprocessor deities. Eight monitors were in emergency states: some were dead, some were fuzzy and delirious. Four small servers were suffering from senility: forgetting where they were, what they were doing, their hard drives, their BIOS, their memory and identity. In a ward filled with electronic suffering, Jimmy played a junior doctor buried in the despair of an epidemic. Before you could say 'malpractice' another drive would die and Jimmy was crying. If he had time, his much-vaunted logic might have realised that a strong magnetic force was sabotaging his efforts, but he had no time: he had to save what he could.

And most heartbreaking of all was a screen where red dots were supposed to turn blue, and the parking system for the hospital was supposed to be monitored and modelled and someday modified. Now the blue flashed on and off like Christmas lights and persistence of vision made them appear to be stuck in a pattern not unlike a serpent coiled around a nine pointed star, but like the dot-to-dot look of the night sky, you could see any pattern you wanted if you spent enough time looking for it, but Jimmy was not inclined to look.

Eventually Lynn and Violet came out of the hospital door and Bog leant forward from the Portacabin and propelled himself towards them. This was Jimmy's nadir: from this point on, he managed to secure some data and some screens were recovered. Perhaps this too is a coincidence.

'Did you do what you had to do?' asked Lynn, in a tone of voice that hinted that she did not appreciate Bog's secrecy.

'Yeah.'

'Dan said goodbye…' said Violet.

'Yeah?'

'Well, he waffled on about Sir Isaac Newton's magical studies at Cambridge and claimed he was some sort of alchemical wedding-singer… but we assumed that was his way of saying goodbye!'

'Oh,' Said Bog.

'So where did you park the car?' asked Violet with joky trepidation.

There was a pause whilst Violet's joke lost its humour.

'Um...' said Bog. 'Give me a second! I know I parked somewhere close!'

They had driven to the hospital via the River Cam, where they had thrown out a container's worth of water and soaked paper. Bog had stopped the car and let Violet and Lynn out whilst he drove round and round the car park in search of a parking space. Although many of the pagans claimed access to second-sight, it was hindsight that was a particular group-strength, and Lynn was as much annoyed with herself as with Bog. She should have stayed in the car. She should not have trusted the idiot with remembering where he had parked. Bog never remembered anything to do with cars. She should have known.

They walked around the main car park for several minutes. Then they walked to some of the other car parks and strolled up and down the rows of cars there. All the time, Bog was walking a strange two-steps-forward-one-step-to-the-side walk whilst behind him Violet and Lynn were muttering curses and staring daggers at his back. Eventually though they had to accept that the car was lost and they were going home by bus. This did not seem to worry Bog too much. He was used to it, but Lynn had gone beyond angry mutterings to sullen grumblings and the bus trip back was filled with dark silences and accusatory glances. It took two hours to get back to the house. If Bog knew where he had parked the car, it would probably have taken twenty minutes.

Life at the house was continuing at a much more relaxed pace. The four men had spent the last few hours arranged amongst the pillows in the front room, each surrounded by little piles of books and notes and pens and pencils. Every so often the silence was broken as they would discuss what they were reading and occasionally they would break for a cup of tea or coffee, made with incredible diligence lest the kitchen was messed up. No one wanted to anger the surprisingly house-proud Bog.

At one point, Michael had wandered down to the corner shop to stock up on 'essentials'; muesli, wine and rolling tobacco, and had wandered back with these, plus the usual joss-sticks that the owner of the shop always managed to sell him. Michael didn't need any joss sticks. He had a cupboard in the kitchen full of them, but the shop-keeper was very persistent and always feigned a lack of understanding when Michael tried to explain his incense surplus. The owner's skin colour and accent suggested that he was from India, but despite Michael's interest in such matters, he had never ascertained whether the owner's faith was Hindu, Muslim, Buddhist or Goan Christian. What he did know was that the owner's religion did not prohibit him from making money from selling scented candles and joss sticks to stupid white heathens. Michael would send Gavyn next time, he thought.

When Michael got back he put the groceries tidily away in the kitchen and then resumed his untidy sprawl amongst the books and cushions in the front room. He asked Kelly, Gavyn and Enschol Bralcht about their studies and found it very reassuring that after four days the group were starting to work as a team and thinking along similar lines. Everyone seemed to have compatible ideas and comparable thoughts about the exorcism. It was almost as if they were all being controlled by a single mind. Everyone's notepads were filling up with notes from the various books that they were devouring: everyone but Enschol Bralcht whose notepad was unblemished, probably because written English was not his strongpoint.

If you were to study the three blemished notepads you might notice that occasionally the handwriting changed from the flowing scripts of Kelly, Michael and Gavyn to a more stilted calligraphy. In fact, there were times when the three wrote things down that they had no conscious memory of writing. Kelly thought that this must be a form of automatic writing and he had found a way to tap into a large and universal pool of intelligence. Michael thought that his old age was making him absent-minded. Gavyn was the only one who was suspicious that this might mean something else, but as he couldn't work out what the 'something else' was, he eventually accepted his two divergent writing styles as a fact without further meaning. Meanwhile Enschol Bralcht was so quiet that he was almost invisible.

The curious calm of the readers was eventually shattered by the loud opening of the front door, the noisy stomping of sulky feet and the corresponding slam of the door behind Violet, Lynn and Bog. Perhaps here was the clearest proof for the existence of auras; because before they had even left the hallway and made it into the front room, Michael knew that they were not happy.

He stood up with a guilty spurt of energy. He did not believe he had any reason to feel guilty, but when you've been feeling calm and relaxed and you are met by a friend or colleague who is stressed or miserable, a rogue guilty feeling erupts unchecked by reason. As Violet, Bog and Lynn entered, Michael had already started to recite an old charm to diffuse antagonism:

'Cuppa tea?' he said, and although the world was still far from right, the phrase resounded through the air and began to dissolve the tense atmosphere that the newcomers had brought with them into the house.

'Yeah. We could do with one,' said Violet. She smiled faintly as she made her way to where Gavyn was sitting amongst the books and pillows.

Bog was taking all the comments and sly looks as personal attacks upon his nature. He accepted that his lack of affection for his four-wheeled vehicle was a particular peccadillo of his and that upon this occasion it had caused a small problem for other people, but he had given them a lift to the hospital without receiving any thanks and he would have driven them back (if he could have located his car) with no complaint. They were ungrateful and petty minded and pessimistic. They saw a half-empty glass where others might have seen a half-full one, and in conclusion they were bloody lucky that they hadn't had to take the bus there, as well as back.

Bog, stooping in a sulk, stormed past Michael (on his way to the kitchen) and continued to the Entropy Room. His pace increased as he went down the hall and then there was a moment of transcendental and brutal beauty.

There is a part of a ballet, as the feather-light ballerina launches herself into the air, when she appears to hover for a second, (despite our preconceptions about gravity), before she descends into the waiting arms of a young, muscular man in unfeasibly tight stockings. This segment of stylised dance was replicated almost exactly in the pagan house in Cherry Hinton. Replicated in so far as a man of imagination might just be able to replace the feather-light ballerina with the stocky form of a flying Bog and the arms of a muscular young man with the balsa wood coffee-table and cabinet of the Entropy room. Bog had choreographed his movements to produce the maximum effect and when he came down to earth within a plume of wood-dust and debris, a man of imagination could almost hear the crowds stand up in the stalls and applaud the dance.

In the kitchen, Michael and Lynn heard a loud crash and a dull thump; the two noises simultaneously merging to a 'crump'. Neither of them seemed too concerned about this. Michael's plan was to console one person at a time and whilst he made tea in his unnaturally clean kitchen, he asked Lynn what had happened.

'What happened?' Lynn repeated. 'What happened is that the idiot we were travelling with forgot where he parked his bloody car again...'

'...and how was Dan?' said Michael in his most calming voice.

'Oh...uh...he was fine. He's talking now.'

'What did you talk about?'

'Well, he didn't really talk to us... I think he was talking to an invisible passenger on his tour bus, but it was good to see that his memory wasn't affected by his stroke.'

'How was the ward? Was it tidy? Did Dan seem comfortable?'

For a woman who was paid by the local authorities as a counsellor, Lynn was as susceptible to psychological tricks as anyone, and Michael's insistence that Lynn talk about what really mattered (Dan and not Bog), appeared to relax her. She was starting to be persuaded that the story in her head about the selfish idiot Bog was really a story about the convalescing Dan, with Bog's missing car as just one of a number of details. Whenever Lynn mentioned Bog with any aggression, Michael reminded her of an old adage that he was fond of, about reconsidering those acts that you first thought of as malicious as merely being thoughtless.

By the time the kettle had boiled and the tea was made Lynn was talking more freely, with less anger and more humour: perhaps it was the effect of the tea fumes. She told Michael about the ward, about the nurses and doctors and of her triumph over an evil Christian evangelist. She carried on talking as they made their way back into the front room with tea for Violet. Then Michael left Lynn to chat with the rest of the group while he took a cup of tea into the Entropy Room to see if he could calm Bog.

Bog was sitting in the middle of a pile of wreckage with a look of exhaustion on his face. He had already relieved enough aggression upon the furnishings to make the 'magic of tea' redundant, but nonetheless Michael passed him the cup in a spirit of camaraderie and fairness, and they talked briefly about Dan. After Michael said something to Bog about malice, misinterpretations and ignorance, they both left the Entropy Room to rejoin the others.

Enschol Bralcht was quiet. This was not unusual: the dark foreigner was never the most vocal member of the group. He was so quiet that the lack of sound was accompanied by a lack of presence. He was barely in the room at all. Again, this was not unusual. There is however a problem with the word 'unusual'. If we measure what is 'usual' by our expectations of what is possible in our mundane and science-shackled world, then Enschol Bralcht was weird. However, if you take the oddity of a resurrectionist as a fact, his actions are all predictable and his motivations understandable. Poor Enschol Bralcht.

123

Next to Enschol Bralcht, (or what remained of his physical presence), was Kelly. Strange Kelly, as he was still called behind his back, was playing the role of buffer between Enschol Bralcht and reality. No one noticed the disappearance of the foreigner whilst Kelly's presence existed as an irritation at the periphery of everyone else's vision. Enschol Bralcht knew all there was to know about Kelly and like everyone else, he didn't particularly like what he knew.

Lynn was thinking about Bog and about Michael, whom she thought would make a marvellous counsellor. There was something inside Lynn that was examining these thoughts and was surprised to find that Lynn was aware of its existence. The something left her quickly though: before Lynn had time to pinpoint what it was. Perhaps because she felt threatened by 'the something' or perhaps because she was still annoyed at having to take a bus home from Addenbrokes, she began complaining again.

'If it had been anyone but one of you guys I would have set a golem on him.'

This was the sort of boastful non sequitur that would be more at home coming from Kelly's mouth. Everyone let her rant without further comment, but Gavyn couldn't help remembering that golems were mud-men created using a trick of the Hebrew language where, with the addition or deletion of one letter, the word for dirt could be transformed into the word for life. It was a trick that allegedly could be performed only by particular Jewish rabbis. Gavyn knew that

Lynn was not Jewish and as rabbis were all men, it was doubtful that she could carry out this threat. This was the problem with modern pagans: they knew enough about alternative mythologies to sound exotic but not enough to be plausible. However, anyone who knew Lynn knew that she was surrounded by bad luck. She had what psychologists sometimes refer to as a 'victim mentality' which meant that any small problem that came her way would grow into a catastrophe before too long. What would happen therefore, thought Gavyn, if she could direct this force onto someone else? Why not suppose that this was possible? And if this were possible why not call this force golem or vampire or shadow, or any number of monster names?

Meanwhile a monster by the name of Enschol Bralcht was creeping through a backdoor in Gavyn's head. It didn't get far though before it faced another door or a wall or a rampart and ditch. Gavyn was a defensive individual. He gave little away. Once, a long time ago, when he'd been a student, he had opened up his mind to a stage hypnotist and had been too embarrassed by this to risk this kind of honesty ever again. Gavyn hated being let down by his heart or head. But still the monster found a path through the labyrinth to a part of Gavyn that thought of Michael as a good man: foolish and fickle but a good and charming man.

From Gavyn to Violet was a natural and easy step: the two were linked. There are some modern scientific theories that say that at a quantum level the borders of a human being are a lot blurrier than we normally accept, and people who live together are like twin suns with belts of atomic matter in strange orbits around and between them. If Enschol Bralcht followed Gavyn's thought for too long in any direction he could not help but end up at Violet. Once inside Violet, however, Enschol Bralcht was lost, or to be more precise he was hit by a powerful wave of culture shock. From the walled city inside Gavyn's head, he arrived unequipped for the wide open spaces of Violet's psyche. She was so open, so willing to accept, so broad in scope and yet so shifting in idea space. There were no fixed points of reference. She was psychically very similar to Michael, but she did not have his learning, his house or the respect that he had built up and fed by the pagan community. Enschol Bralcht liked the learning and the house and the respect. He moved on.

All these little journeys were easy for Enschol Bralcht. All the destinations were visible to him. All of the victims sat before him, lined up like cardboard ducks at a fairground shooting range. Now, however, he was going to try a longer-range shot and with no physical visibility of the target: a piece of psychic sniping with a blacked-out telescopic lens. He was going after Bog.

Lying amongst the broken balsa, Bog was talking with Michael, but for short periods of time he found himself drifting from the conversation; not listening but simply thinking about the grey haired yet youthfully enthusiastic pagan role model who crouched before him. Bog was impressed by the calm way that Michael handled situations. He was never angry and seldom upset. There were still problems in his past that needed exorcising, but he was genuinely a good man with far fewer pretensions than the average pagan. Bog also liked Michael as a friend and treated him like a soul-mate. Bog had a particular weakness that meant he could not face the world without someone else to drink with or to talk to. He was not a social person. Many thought of him as an anti-social person and it was true that in general his opinion of humanity was limbo low. However there is a saying that 'no man is an island' and Bog always seemed to form an attachment with someone and for the past three years that someone had been Michael. No man is an island and Bog was a peninsular.

Enschol Bralcht learned much from Bog and with his confidence rising he risked straying even further from his fading body.

Old Dan was asleep or drugged or both, and he was rambling through a tour of his city again. He was thinking of Kit Marlow. He was thinking of a young student in the Cambridge of the sixteenth century. Not yet the toast of London's theatregoers, Kit was already being courted by Walsingham, the Queen's spymaster. This was the age of the first Cold War: a war between the Papists and the Protestants. From the reclaimed flatlands of the Fens to the sodden lowlands of Europe he travelled and made connections and relayed messages. The flatlands were the same, whether in the Netherlands or Cambridgeshire: they were dark and damp and attracted disease and distrust.

Centuries later, Cambridge was still the chosen centre for British treachery. During the Second World War, a parachuting Dutchman called Wulf Schmidt was captured in Willingham and spent the rest of the war feeding the Germans false intelligence. After the war, nearby Godmanchester was used as the safe house for Heisenberg and Germany's Nuclear scientists, and every room was safely insulated with microphones in the walls and floors and ceilings, and all through this period Kim Philby, Guy Burgess, Donald MacLean and Anthony Blunt sold their country's secrets to an appreciative Russia.

Later still, in a room in St. Johns College, a young man is dying. There is something of a ritual about his death: a shiny blessed blade lies beside him, glinting beneath the blood and the water.

Enschol Bralcht pulled back into his body with a start. This wasn't like his experience with Lynn. This wasn't a consciousness trying to seek out an invading entity. This was an unconscious part of Dan's mind reacting to the presence of Enschol Bralcht. That part of Dan knew about Enschol Bralcht from the start. Why else would it be thinking of spies? Why else would it concentrate on treachery and the enemy within? Why else did it end in a room in St. John's College?

Enschol Bralcht was experiencing a new feeling: fear.

128

He did not like it. Dan knew too much and could prevent Enschol Bralcht from fulfilling his destiny. Poor Enschol Bralcht. He hadn't even quizzed Dan about his thoughts on Michael.

Chapter Seven:
Uneasy Shuffling

'Would you like some reassurance for tomorrow, Michael?' asked Lynn.

Michael looked at her quizzically. He was always open to help, suggestion and friendship, but he didn't fully understand what she was talking about until he saw the pack of cards that she had taken from her handbag.

'Tarot? Why not?' he said, walking back into the room with a particularly dusty Bog shadowing him.

Lynn ushered Michael to her, and pulled a pillow from a pile and placed it in front of her. He dutifully sat down and with everyone reverentially gathering around the dealer and the dealee, she asked him to cut the cards a few times and then dealt a circular pattern between them.

It was a clock: a pagan time machine set twenty four hours into the future. The interesting cards lay at eleven and eight o'clock and showed 'The World' (a good omen of worldly success... Enschol Bralcht smiled) and 'The Hanged Man (reversed)' (which was all about trials and tests, according to Lynn). The upside down hanged man looked amusing to Gavyn, and he said so to the group.

'It looks like someone doing the Indian rope trick: the old fakir trick where you follow a rope up into thin air'.

'Yes,' said the collective voice, unsure whether this was a comment of great depth about the future or a sarcastic observation about the random and meaningless symbols on the cards.

The other ten cards were the usual statistical distribution of cups, coins, swords and staves. Lynn had less to say about these 'minor arcana' but still, everyone was impressed by her apparent knowledge and her memory of the hundred and fifty two meanings.

'Is that OK?' asked Lynn staring Michael directly in the eyes. It was the tone of a mother to a child, with the slight hint that she was willing to change the future if he didn't like it.

'Yeah. I guess so. It seems that there will be some tribulations but it'll all be fine in the end'.

Gavyn, the class sceptic, was never willing to accept the non-specific nature of fortune telling. It always seemed vague and the recipient always seemed so undemanding. He was an odd sort of sceptic though, because although he doubted fortune-tellers' abilities, he had no problem accepting that in an infinite universe the chance of there really being individuals who could predict the future was perfectly acceptable to him. It was similar to his feelings about aliens. He found it easy to believe that somewhere in the vastness of space there were non-terrestrial life-forms, but he did not believe the drunken retarded kissing-cousins who were regularly interviewed for American television about their abductions by quizzical Martians with an unnatural interest in the population of trailer-park dwellers in Kansas. Gavyn put Lynn to the test.

'Would you tell my fortune?' he asked, interrupting the too-long stare that Lynn had held with Michael. Having an audience and being the centre of attention was not antagonistic to her, so she agreed. To prove that she was not a 'one-trick-pony', however, she dealt the cards in a cross pattern this time; although her particular religious bigotry meant that she called it 'two lines meeting at a central point' instead. At first, there was nothing of particular interest for Gavyn, in fact there were no major arcana and only a smattering of court cards, but to answer specific questions Lynn dealt more cards upon those already showing and it didn't take too long before 'The Moon' card appeared. This was Gavyn's test. Perhaps it showed that he was as superstitious and fuzzy-minded as any of the group, but he always seemed to get 'The Moon' card and now considered it as 'his card'. Of course, there is a coincidence factor at play here, but if 'The Moon' didn't rise in Cherry Hinton, he would have forever thought of Lynn as a fake. An unfair trial of witchcraft perhaps, but at least it didn't involve a ducking stool.

Now the floodgates had metaphorically been opened. Everyone in the room had opinions about prediction and they all knew of a number of techniques to shake a little future from the randomness of the present. After the Tarot cards had been packed away, Bog tried his hand at reading tea leaves: an old gypsy trick of searching for meaning in the scum at the bottom of the cup. However, it was only halfway through a reading with the surprisingly naïve Kelly that Bog had to admit that he knew nothing about reading the leaves and had just started the whole pantomime as a way of getting Michael to make them all a cup of tea. Everyone thought this was hilarious; even Michael, who punctuated his laughing with short phrases insinuating doubts about Bog's parentage.

The lightening of the mood, however, did not quell people's interests in divination. It was a school of magic that everyone had delved into at one stage or another. Other forms of magic (conjuration, invocation or enchantment) had sinister overtones and some people were wary about their associations with otherworldly entities, but few saw the harm in a little fortune-telling. And so, once the tea reading jokes had dissipated, Violet offered to give Michael a psychic second opinion via the I Ching.

She knew how to get the readings, but she did not

have the memory that Lynn had, so asked Michael to get his copy of the book. Then she placed three coins in Michael's hand and asked him to meditate upon the future events before throwing the coins on a pillow between them. He did this a number of times until Violet was able to build up a six-lined reading: the hexagram. Then she read the interpretation from the book: 'Integrity. Success. Righteous persistence brings reward...' It was all good stuff.

'Fortune Cookie homilies,' said a derisory Bog, but Violet defended her chosen scrying method by explaining that unlike Tarot, the I Ching did not presume to tell of the future but instead hinted at the best way to cope with the future when it came. She then continued with her reading, elaborating on the 'changing lines' just as Lynn had elaborated by adding cards at various moments to her initial patterns. The 'changing lines', explained Violet, were those that were neither fully Yin nor Yang, but undecided, fence-sitting grey hermaphrodite questions in a black-and-white universe. Gavyn joined in, explaining that Violet also had another few methods of reading coins and yarrow sticks and other oriental nic-nacs, but they were all similar in interpretation and all apparently could be traced to marks on bone when it split in fires or patterns on turtles' backs. Michael suggested that this was due to the aura of wisdom and longevity that surrounds turtles like a shell. Bog suggested it was because it's easier to study the backs of wild turtles than the backs of wild jackrabbits. They were probably both right.

The conversation ebbed and flowed across the room: Lynn talked about seeing the future in dreams whilst Enschol Bralcht, (poor quiet Enschol Bralcht), surprised everyone by talking about the old practice of reading the future in the entrails of birds and mammals. Then the cups of tea were replaced with glasses of wine and the volume and enthusiasm of the conversation rose to new heights. At one stage Bog went upstairs to his room and returned with a small silk bag full of cards. The initial response of cautious or fake interest in Bog's Tarot deck changed into a very enthusiastic and real interest as the squat biker explained that these were not Tarot at all. These were all he had left of a set of cards that he designed with a friend of his; when they got bored of Tarot's dogmatic and simplistic symbology. They had instead made, (and very well made — they had a friend in a printing shop), a set of eighty-three slightly surreal images with no prescriptive explanation. What you see, you interpret: WYSYI ('wizz-ee-ee' as Bog called his rule).

This of course is a post modern cartomancy, alluding to the computer programmer's magic word 'WYSIWIG' (wiz-ee-wig) — what you see is what you get.

If only Bog's cards were that clear: what you saw was an intricate cut away picture of a heart straight out of 'Gray's Anatomy' with telephones in two of the four chambers and the word 'Telepathy' written along the bottom. One of the other cards had a flaming bowler hat and the words 'Cricket Match' on it. Bog had fifty beautifully designed cards that were as surreal and as calculated as The Times crossword. Alan (Bog's friend) was a big fan of The Times crossword, although he had never actually completed one of those cryptomantic nightmares.

Bog suspected that Alan still had the missing thirty-three cards. There were plenty of cards he remembered but had not seen for years. Where was 'The Accountant', 'The Cheese Plate' or 'The Two of Shades'?

Lynn, who was usually known for treating 'The Craft' too seriously, even relaxed enough to give Michael a test-reading with Bog's cards. The interpretation (as agreed by the whole group) was thought to be favourable: 'The Chocolate Biscuit' could not be anything but a good omen and, combined with 'The Joy Rider', suggested a stolen biscuit; which everyone agreed was the best tasting biscuit of all.

While Kelly excused himself and went upstairs, Bog explained how anyone could make a non-prescriptive divination pack from raiding the toy boxes of Charity Shops for Children's card games; after all, what is the true psychological interpretation of 'Mr Bun the Baker' from the 'Happy Family' game or the 'Goat' from 'Farmyard Snap, for children aged three and above'?

Bog also answered Gavyn's question about why there were eighty-three cards in Bog's original pack. The number was a prime number but apart from that, to Bog's knowledge it had no mystical associations. '...And that's the whole point: the pack has no baggage, no history and no external associations. Wizz-ee-ee.', insisted Bog.

Then Kelly came back with his pack of cards. By this time it was getting harder and harder to show enthusiasm for some assorted pieces of laminated cardboard. Kelly's pack was a Tarot deck, but like Bog he'd designed it himself, along the lines of the prediction cards that parapsychologists used to test telepathy. Thus they were all classic Tarot designs simplified to their logical extremes of a couple of lines, circles, curves, rectangles and the occasional stick figure that seemed quite comical and suggested the real reason for Kelly's deck: his inability to draw.

Although less warmly received than Bog's odd cards, Kelly's deck stirred up a debate that lasted well into the night and well into the ninth bottle of wine. Kelly argued that having simplified the images, he had made the cards less pictorial and your response to them was thus more immediate and empathic and emotional, rather the cerebral exercise of remembering what each card meant. Bog, on the other hand, argued that the cards were still prescriptive and the simplified images only highlighted exactly which symbols were supposed to mean what, according to the books. Meanwhile out of Kelly's earshot a crueller conversation was going on between Lynn and Violet about how sad and silly these stickmen cards were. The strange thing was that, as the night flowed onwards, the arguments were still raging at fever-pitch, but Bog and Kelly had appeared to have completely swapped sides. Bog forced his opinion that the cards contained more freedom in their simplicity and Kelly argued that he designed them to be stricter and more controlled versions of designs that had gotten too elaborate to interpret correctly. Meanwhile, Gavyn, staring at a large circle hanging luminously above a wavy line that began and ended with two small upward facing arcs, was happy and drunk and surprisingly fond of Kelly's bad drawings.

Gavyn shut his eyes for a while (his eyelids were already a little heavy from the red wine, which had been flowing from the bottle to his glass and into his mouth) and clarified his universe into Kelly-like simplicity. To one side of him two stick figures were arguing; round mouth-holes opening and closing rapidly in the similar round rings that represented their heads. One of the figures had a thicker squatter frame than the other: one was made of plastic straws and one was made of lead pipes. He turned his head and saw his partner, Violet, as a set of sexily proportioned curved lines. He saw Michael-stick-figure and Lynn-stick-figure, and he saw an Enschol-Bralcht-stick-figure, which either his conscious or unconscious mind had decided to make a little blurry about its lines. No one could quite get a grasp on who Mr. Bralcht was or anything about his personality. Poor Enschol Bralcht: it couldn't be easy for a foreigner to understand normal spoken English, and much less the complex philosophical and metaphysical debates that the pagan group favoured.

This reminded Gavyn of something Michael had told him (Michael being the less curvaceous stick figure between the two more voluptuous ones). Gavyn had once asked Michael why he thought so many of the apparently wisest people were the biggest non-conformists. Why this group, for instance, was comprised of bikers and hippies and dopeheads and others who could be stereotyped as anything but the norm. Michael paused for thought, or for dramatic effect, and then told Gavyn that it was as if life was a giant centrifuge and thus all of the most massive souls are thrown to the edges of society. It was a great analogy... although it was probably bollocks!

Gavyn regretted that memory almost as soon as he had regurgitated it. Kelly had been offering his strange cigarettes around and the effects of a few puffs of one of these, plus a large amount of red wine combined with the gyratory image made Gavyn feel quite nauseous. Gavyn, being a quiet and discrete fellow, decided that vomiting all over the front room was impolite so excused himself and made his way through the kitchen to the back door and the fresh air of the garden. This helped. He felt a little self-conscious sitting on his own on the back step staring into the night, while everyone else was talking loudly about predictions, but he would rather feel self-conscious and embarrassed than ill.

After a while, to occupy his mind (and stop it from

dwelling in an alcohol-induced vertigo) he began to stare at the pots of dandelions that sat either side of the doorway. He'd never really looked at dandelions before. Oh sure, he knew what they looked like and had pulled a fair few out of his own lawn in an effort to teach those weeds a good lesson about horticultural trespassing, but he'd never really looked at them as objects of nature's beauty the way that Michael had.

They really were quite beautiful plants. Disc-shaped flower-heads and long stems separating the garish flower from the green base of leaves. Gavyn thought that they were not unlike the carnations that populated the garden before Michael chopped down the apple-tree and planted his weeds. But with Gavyn's drug-addled mind, he couldn't quite think of a beautiful description to match the beautiful object. The flower was not an 'eruption' of colour. The concentric arrangement of tiny petals was too uniform to be volcanic. Carnation flowers were eruptions: they were random frills and spills of pink and white flesh. The name meant 'of-the-flesh' or 'physical'. The dandelion flower was something else: an explosion of fiery petals? No, that wasn't right. An explosion would involve a pattern of petals that was condensed at the centre and sparser at the edges, as the kinetic power was dissipated and the shock wave died. He struggled to find the thesaurus in his brain: 'A floral fiesta', 'A solar disc', 'A Busby Berkley Choreography of a Plant'?

Finally he found a description he liked: a mandala. It all made sense. It was intricate and detailed and compact and multi-layered. It was also the same yellow-orange of a Buddhist monk's saffron robes. *Oh wow!* he thought at this epiphany. *I've got to tell Violet about this.*

Luckily his unsteady legs gave him a moment's pause and enough time to decide against this course of action. Although it was true that discovering Buddha amongst the flowers would appeal to Violet, (in the right situation), nothing shows up how drunk you are, to your friends and colleagues, as well as trying to call your partner out to a garden in the middle of the night to show her a religious allegory.

Perhaps, I'll tell her later, he thought.

'What are you looking at,' asked Violet, standing quietly behind him, 'Are you alright?'

Meanwhile, and at the exact same time, a nurse was leaning over Old Dan's bed and asking, 'Are you alright?'

This moment of synchronicity, (a compassionate sympathetic multi-loci echo), could be thought of as proof that magic, in some wonderfully real way, existed. However, no one could be in both places at the same time to check stop-watches and switch on tape-recorders, so if this was magic's scream for attention, it went unnoticed.

'I was dreaming. I think I was dreaming', repeated Old Dan.

'What were you dreaming about', asked the nurse nonchalantly; no doubt expecting the vague answer of a man who was cautiously crawling towards consciousness after a

142

four day break.

'…I was dreaming of trouble-makers…of Kit Marlow who upset both Catholics and Protestants when the religions were drawing battle-lines… of George Gordon, who as Lord Byron, upset the moralists of his age…of Edward Crowley who proved a similar barbarian to his society and to a man I used to know called Enschol Bralcht who upset me. Have you ever met anyone who even when they know the rules, refuse to accept them?'

'Mm-hmm' murmured the nurse in a non-committal way. 'Now. Drink up your water and lie back and I'll go fetch the doctor and tell him you're awake.'

Having had the rules defined, Dan obeyed. You don't get to his age by swimming against the prevailing current.

'I don't like rules.' confessed Michael. 'I don't like timetables and structures and goals and destinations. I prefer to journey without fixed destinations and find myself in surprising new places that only random fate could destine for. However, it's come to my attention,' he looked at Enschol Bralcht and Bog, 'that as this week is drawing to its close and a psychic crescendo emerges, (despite my best efforts not to plan one), I should tell you what I think we should do tomorrow, and if you have any opinions or additions to this, then please tell me. This is a democracy after-all,' said the unofficial and unelected king of the pagan community. 'Tomorrow, if we get up early enough, we'll go for a road trip to one of the most sacred sites in Cambridgeshire; Wandlebury.' He paused, for dramatic effect or to let the others comment. As no comments were forthcoming, he continued. 'I'll need one of you to pick up the group photos of us, so that at the end of the day you can all have a souvenir of your pagan retreat week. Then after a picnic at Wandlebury, we'll come back to the house for the afternoon's ritual exorcism. Then I expect there will be drinking and cavorting into the night, a good breakfast on Saturday morning and then you can all go home, refreshed and energised from a week of education, enlightenment and mutual support... How does that sound?'

It was true that Michael disliked plans. The world is an ever-changing place, and there are so many things that could ruin even the best-laid-plans that Michael did not see the point in making them in the first place. Now, however, he had foretold the future; he felt strangely powerful. He had overcome one of his entrenched character traits and this seemed an appropriate start to an exorcism of his past life. He was a new man: he made decisions, his own decisions, and even though it had taken Enschol Bralcht and Bog to persuade him to take this unprecedented step, Michael felt like a man in charge of his own destiny.

There were questions about what they'd be doing in Wandlebury, which Michael answered with a paternal but patronising 'What would you like to do?', but most people were happy to get any sort of plan out of Michael, and so in groups of two or three they began to disappear upstairs to their rooms to sleep. The last to go was Enschol Bralcht, who seemed to want to stay up a while longer than the rest of them to gloat on his successful manipulation of Michael. In fact, he alone did not disappear upstairs to sleep for fear that he would disappear altogether and he was too close to his goal to let that happen.

Friday was a good day: an auspicious day, thought Michael. His alarm clock was programmed to wake him up by switching on the radio to a particular commercial channel. This wasn't because he liked the station's choice of music, (quite the opposite), or the amusing and intelligent banter of the DJs, (they were all dull and insultingly ignorant). However, he had found throughout his working life, (when alarms and clocks and timetables had meant something to him), that he could sleep through an electronic bleeping alarm, but certain radio stations were so cringingly awful that he had to wake up to switch them off.

The radio station, however, was currently the emissary of his high expectations. The weatherman, (as selfishly jovial and inane as the DJ that introduced him), was predicting the weather for the country and it was Michael's weather: the weather that made him happy.

A long time ago, Michael realised that the merits of meteorology were arbitrary. People, without thinking, would say that a sunny day was 'good' or a rainy day 'bad' and yet if they were questioned further by a persistent Michael they had to admit that one sort of weather could be hotter, colder, wetter, drier or any number of useful comparisons, but not 'better'. If an award system could be worked out for the local atmosphere, then who would be its judge or judging panel and would underachieving weather that failed to get an award one year, try even harder to gain a gold at the next weather-Olympics. It seemed unlikely.

The other oddity that Michael had noticed about the merits of meteorology was that the undefined classification system, which the unconscious mind used, appeared to be culturally biased. In this way a farmer in the fens thought a rainy day in Summer was good and beneficial, a yachtsman in The Wash knew that dry windy days were the best, and in Cambridge itself, the cyclists navigating through the traffic like brave Spaniards at a bull-run, asked the gods for 'nice, cool dry weather'. Michael also found it amusing how many Englishmen, upon seeing the first flurry of snow falling to the welcoming ground, felt their hearts leap as nostalgia rejuvenated them to their childhoods with memories of snowball fights and sledges and cancelled school-lessons. It is only later, when the snow settles, that the cold damp reality of digging out cars, slippery and treacherous paths and increased heating bills kill the nostalgia and the children grow up fast.

So Michael, knowing that good weather was arbitrary and culturally biased, in an effort to remake himself a strong and independent man, re-trained his mind to feel that snow-

146

flurry-joy from a previously unheralded weather. Like Michael's promotion of weeds in his garden, his happiness at hearing 'Fifteen degrees centigrade, dry and with a slight Southerly breeze' was purposely at odds with society, but no less wonderful.

He dressed quickly and bounded downstairs, with a child's urgency to go out and play. He skidded on the tiled floor, turning the corner into the hallway and made a grand entrance into the kitchen where Gavyn and Violet and Enschol Bralcht were waiting for him; the first two eating bowls of cereal and the latter torturing a piece of toast. Perhaps 'fifteen degrees centigrade, dry and with a slight Southerly breeze' was good weather for everyone, because Michael's smile was echoed by Gavyn and Violet and far more surprisingly, Enschol Bralcht. In fact, his grin was his best so far. Usually his expression was blank and unreadable, but today, for some reason, he seemed to have mastered the smile that he'd been struggling with all week and although he still had oddly forgettable features, his smile was visually persistent even when his face faded.

Over the next hour the kitchen filled with the chaos that can be expected when seven people all want to eat different things and talk rubbish whilst others try to squeeze past to reach for marmalade or the sugar bowl. In this chaos, however, certain things became clear: certain flaws or amendments to Michael's plan.

Michael knew this would happen. This was the last

147

time that he'd ever plan anything: 'action through non-action', 'go with the flow', 'obey your own nature'; these were the homilies that spoke to Michael with the truest of voices. He should have listened.

The problem, (despite Michael's despair), was not an insurmountable one. His plan involved everyone going to Wandlebury for the morning. Seven people would fit comfortably into two cars and the Gog Magog Hills, (named after the two giants that protected the sacred site and the nearby profane golf course), were only a couple of miles away. However, what Michael had forgotten last night was that although he knew where his car was, Bog's vehicle was lost, somewhere near Addenbrookes.

A new plan was hastily put together and Gavyn somehow became its spokesman or 'shoutsman' as he had to raise his voice over the top of less-constructive conversations to tell everyone that he or Michael would drive Michael's car and ferry everybody to Wandlebury in two journeys: everybody but Bog, who would pick up the group photographs and then proceed on his own holy quest for the missing vehicle. They would exchange mobile phone numbers and Bog would join the rest of the group in the Gog Magog Hills when (and if) he recovered his car. Otherwise, he'd rejoin everyone at the house, after lunch.

The less-constructive conversations included Enschol Bralcht and Michael talking about the history of Wandlebury, (they could have had that conversation later), Violet and Lynn talking about what they usually had for breakfast, (they could have had that conversation quieter), and Bog and Kelly talking about underwear, (they could have avoided that conversation altogether and the world would not have been a worse place for its omission).

The theory went something like this: there was an idea, that both Bog's mother and Kelly's had forced into them at an early age. They were both told that they had to ensure that when they left the house, they had clean underwear on, in case they were involved in an accident and the arriving ambulance crew had to pull them from the wreckage and, for some unspecified surgical reasons, remove their trousers. The fear was that if a paramedic discovered a little boy with dirty pants, he would carefully place the youngster back in the wreckage and drive on; disgusted.

Violet and Lynn, interrupting their own conversation about what fruit went with which cereal, (as well as Gavyn's loud planning), agreed that their mothers had also shared this advice with them. Bog and Kelly, however, took this piece of motherly wisdom to its sympathetic magical conclusions. If mothers insist that you have clean underwear for when you get hit by a truck, a car, a train or a falling piano, then logically people with dirty underwear do not experience these problems. Hospitals, according to mothers, (who are, after all, goddesses in the eyes of their children), are inhabited solely by people with clean white underpants and thus one unusual and unsavoury way of avoiding hospitals and therefore having perfect health is to have the most disgustingly filthy undergarments in the world. Really smelly underwear could make you practically immortal. If you never changed your underwear, declared Kelly, then not just the paramedics but death himself would not touch you.

Violet, overhearing this conversation, had a horrifying thought that Kelly was just the sort of necromancer who might try this death-defying trick. Enschol Bralcht also overheard this conversation and found it very interesting. Poor Enschol Bralcht.

Chapter Eight:
The Horse's Knees

It took another two hours for breakfasts to be eaten, crockery to be washed and put away and conversations to reach their logical ends. Then Michael got into the car with Gavyn and Violet, (the hastily agreed scouting party for the Wandlebury expedition), while Bog wandered to the photography shop to pick up the group photos and then to the bus stop to begin his quest for the lost four-wheeled vehicle.

At the bus stop, to pass the time before the bus arrived, Bog opened up the pack of photos to see just how bad he looked. A stout man, with tired eyes and tired tattoos, not enough hair on his scalp and too much on his chin, wearing a shabby leather jacket that looked as if it was twenty years old, (because it was), was an unlikely victim of vanity, but nevertheless Bog liked to check his portraits before the rest of the world did. This allowed him to think up excuses or self-mocking jokes to explain why he looked that particular way in a particular photograph. Bog had a theory that despite primitive man's fear that the camera captures your soul, his own beautiful soul, (the part that added charm to his distressed flesh), was the one part of him that never seemed to make its way through the lens. This idea was remarkably similar to a belief that Gavyn held, and if Bog could read minds he'd be amazed at the coincidence. Bog however was not telepathic, and if anyone within the group could read both his and Gavyn's minds then they had not admitted to it.

'That's odd!' said Bog, out loud, and to himself.

The old lady who stood at the other end of the bus stop gave him a querulous glance.

'Sorry,' said Bog. 'Just talking to myself.'

What Bog found odd was not in the first few photos. They showed Michael with a small child on his knee, or with an old woman beside him, or any other variation of family pictures. It was a challenge to your preconceptions when your pagan priest and free-thinker is also shown to be a normal human being with relatives, who visit occasionally and share tea and cake and gossip about absent cousins. This was a challenge to Bog's preconceptions but what made him exclaim 'That's odd!' was amongst the last few pictures: the ones that Michael had taken of the pagan group two days ago. Bog remembered Michael had taken some pictures, and then had rested the old camera on a chair to take some pictures with the automatic timer, which allowed Michael to quickly join the rest of the group so that everyone was in the photo. Yet, there were no pictures with Enschol Bralcht in them. Bog, (a man who was currently travelling to find his forgotten car), accepted that his memory wasn't perfect, and perhaps Enschol Bralcht had taken some of the pictures and was therefore behind the camera for a couple, but he could not believe that Enschol Bralcht had avoided having his picture taken at least once during the eight, nine... ten photographs. There was even a worrying space in front of Gavyn, where Bog thought he remembered Enschol Bralcht was standing during the photo session. If Bog looked closely, he could almost swear that shy Gavyn was trying to duck behind the figure of Bralcht who was not there.

Bog found the gap between scientific evidence and his memory so 'odd' that he really wanted to talk it through with someone and regretted the fact that for the first time in days there were no pagans around who would understand his concerns and could comprehend what they might mean. This of course was arrogance. If Bog was an unlikely victim of vanity, it was the sin of arrogance, (or 'human quirk' of arrogance for those who dislike the Ibrahemic term 'sin'), that attacked Bog and his fellow believers relentlessly. It went with the territory. To have power, you had to have self-belief, and self-belief was often accompanied by the disbelief in others. You were special. You could see spirits. Change the world with the power of your mind. You had raised the hidden curtain and peeked at the workings of the universe.

Normal people wouldn't understand.

At the other end of the bus stop, 'normal' Nettie Robertson, now in her eighties, surely would not understand the things that Bog had seen, or heard or felt. Yet Nettie, when she was a seven year old girl had been visited by an Angel who had stayed at the foot of her bed and and told her that God loved her, during those months when she had doubt. She also had a preternatural ability with buses that ensured whilst 'normal' people like Bog, might have to wait for hours for one to turn up, she had never waited for more than ten minutes in her life.

Across the road, Bob Henry waved to Nettie. Like most people on the streets of Cherry Hinton at this time of day on a working Friday, he was an octogenarian pensioner. Ten years ago he had visited a Spiritualist church where his recently dead wife had told him not to worry. He hadn't worried since. He knew things that 'normal' people would never know. He passed a young mother dragging a scruffy boy, crying, towards the local doctors. The young mother was concerned because she had heard voices when she was a child and had told nobody for fear that the insanity would spread. Her young son would no longer sleep in his own bed and kept getting bruises but said he didn't know who hit him. She was worried. She knew this was not 'normal'.

The doctor was a man of science, (like the other Cambridge doctors Dee and Forman). He had seen a huge black dog prowl his fenland allotment last Christmas. It was

Black Shuck, East Anglia's devil-dog. He was a man of science, but every time he remembered this encounter, every hair on his body stood up and a cold chill like the devil's breath blew across his spine.

Less than ten minutes after the old lady had reached the bus stop, the bus arrived and she and Bog boarded it for the journey to Addenbrookes. The journey seemed quicker than yesterday's bus ride back to Cherry Hinton. Maybe this was due to the fact that Bog wasn't sitting the entire trip with Lynn's accusatory stare boring a hole in the back of his head. Maybe it was because he was in a better mood than yesterday, or maybe it was because he spent the time wondering about how Enschol Bralcht had managed to sneak out of the photographs.

At Addenbrookes, Bog had a cursory search around the main visitors' car park before heading to reception to begin his quest in its proper methodical manner. He had decided to locate his car before he saw Old Dan, just in case anything bad and costly had happened to it. It was not that he had any particular warm feelings for the vehicle itself, but he remembered that he had a bale of hay on the back seat and if someone else got to it before he did the consequences could be disastrous.

At the reception, Bog waited for Jane, (her name emblazoned on a badge on her chest), to finish shuffling some pieces of paper before he politely asked whether anyone had reported a car being left overnight somewhere on the hospital grounds. Jane looked confused. It was a look that particularly suited her face. Anyone approaching the reception area for help or advice could tell from a distance that her face and its accompanying look meant that help or advice were unlikely to be forthcoming. Her face sank a thousand hopes.

'There are lots of cars parked here,' she stated, unsure of why he was asking.

'I mislaid my car yesterday,' Bog confessed. 'I know I parked it somewhere at Addenbrookes, but couldn't find where. Could anyone help me find my car?' It was a polite and precise request. Despite some embarrassment and misdirected anger Bog was proud of his performance.

'What kind of car is it, sir?'

'Shit,' said Bog in an expulsion of air and grief. 'I don't know.'

'You don't know what type of car it is?'

'No.'

Jane thought about this for a while and then asked, 'Have you only recently bought it?'

'Would it be more understandable if I said 'yes'?'

'Yes.'

'Then yes: I have just brought a new car. I can't remember what type, but I parked it here yesterday and now cannot find it.'

'What colour is it?' Jane asked, trying her best to be helpful.

'I don't know.'

'You don't know what colour your car is?'

'No.'

'Are you sure it's your car?'

'Yes.' Bog was still patient, but anger was straining at the leash.

Jimmy Chamberlain had been watching this interaction from the corner of the room, where he was tinkering with a security camera. He recognised Bog as one of the idiotic pagans that he had confronted yesterday. Whether he was still angry about their ignorance or whether a small part of him associated Bog with the bad luck he had with his computer systems could not be ascertained, but Jimmy disliked Bog and enjoyed seeing his proud shoulders slouch further and further to the floor as his body language disclosed that Jane was being as helpful as usual. Jimmy however could not hear the conversation. There were far too many sick people milling around; coughing and complaining. Jimmy was a scientist. Jimmy was curious. He just had to get closer.

'Can I help?' he said, with a supercilious sneer.

Bog turned his head on its muscular neck and looked up to the face of the rude and abrasive security guard. 'Not you as well.' He sighed to himself, wondering which god or goddess he had offended to deserve this.

157

'I'm looking for my car. I parked it here yesterday. I don't know what model it is. I don't know what registration number it is. I don't know what colour it is. I don't know its chassis number, its age, how much I paid for it or when its next MOT is due. I have a mental block about these things, OK! All I know is that I left it here yesterday. These are my car keys, which belong to it. It has a bale of hay on the back seat. It's got four wheels; one in each corner. Can...you...help...me?'

The last sentence was said through gritted teeth. There was an internal dialogue taking place behind those teeth. The old Bog, (the biker who used to get in trouble with the police), was trying to persuade the new Bog, (the mellow and sensible middle-aged ex-biker), that punching someone in the face would make the situation better. It was a very persuasive argument, but the new Bog was just as stubborn as his younger self and his old age had brought him wisdom. There were enough posters in the reception area to warn you of the severity of starting a fight in a hospital. Bog wanted to get his car back. He did not want to go to the police station for the day.

Bog remembered the last time he had enjoyed the hospitality of the Cambridge Constabulary: ironically he had not been the criminal in that instance. He had gone to the station to pick up his old friend, Alan, after he had been arrested for his beliefs. Alan later wrote an erudite letter to Amnesty International complaining that his overnight stay in the cells was tantamount to harassment and that he had been imprisoned because of his alternative beliefs. Amnesty International did not reply to his letter.

The situation that lead up to Alan's arrest began one night in a quiet pub where Alan and Bog had been drinking and discussing physics. Although the pub in general was quiet, (no juke box, few mid-week boozers), Alan and Bog's conversation had been loud and animated. Alan had just read a book on the practical uses of quantum theory. The practical uses were currently all hypothetical and relied on technology making some incredible advances, but with the minimal physics education that Alan had and the great enthusiasm that Alan and Bog shared, this only made the subject more intriguing. The book tended to focus on computing and its limits. Currently, computers tackled a problem in a serial fashion as each electronic switch was either switched on or off in turn until the series could be interpreted into an answer. The book hypothesised that if computer circuits could be made on an atomic scale, (which seemed feasible), and then on a sub-atomic level, quantum physics could be used where a switch was both on and off at the same time. This meant that multiple scenarios could be tested at the same time and computer operations would increase to genius speeds.

What Alan reminded Bog at this time, and promptly forgot later on, was that for some reason, (seldom explained in popular physics books), normal Newtonian physics did not work at subatomic levels, while quantum physics did not work above sub-atomic levels.

'Why?' asked Bog.

'I don't know. The books never tell.'

They discussed the other quirks of quantum theory.

'One of the other quirks of quantum theory,' said Alan 'is that measurements always give a definitive answer. Therefore, as soon as you observe, detect or measure something you've changed it from being in the blurry 'on and off' state to a more decisive 'on *or* off' state. It's just like that Schrödinger's cat analogy, where the cat is both alive and dead in the box, until someone opens the box and looks in. Therefore quantum computers must be careful not to analyse their own workings.'

'If this book is correct,' said Bog, infected by cheap bitter and Alan's enthusiasm, 'and we'll eventually be able to speed up computers via quantum physics then why not use the same theoretical background to speed up other time-consuming tasks.'

'Yes,' said Alan with a glint in his eye that was probably a side-effect of a synapse switching on in his brain. 'Shopping.'

'Shopping?' said Bog, reliably playing straight man to the joke that he knew was coming.

'Yes, shopping. I hate shopping. It's a waste of my time. Shops never have what I need, never mind what I want, and I have to traipse all across town to buy the normal mix of items that I require. So, why can't I go quantum shopping?'

'You mean that shopping on the Internet using a quantum computer will simplify your life?'

'No. What I mean is real physical quantum shopping. If you could somehow avoid observation you could be in two or more places at once and get the shopping over with in a fraction of the time.'

'But you can't avoid being observed. What about other people? What about security cameras?'

'Those are blind eyes: without a brain to register what the image means they're useless. They don't see you. They are looking at the general picture. Your only problem comes if someone who knows you sees you in a shop. Then that someone will register that you are there at that time in that place and your status will be defined like Schrödinger's moggy as the box lid is lifted.'

'What about your own brain: your own mind's eye? You know where you are. You know what you're doing and that knowledge prevents a human being from getting involved in any quantum nonsense.'

Alan smiled and raised his glass as if it held the secret of the universe: 'Drugs.' He said.

'If you're too drunk, spaced or stoned to know where you are or who you are, you can take part in quantum actions with impunity.'

'Till receipts and credit card transactions: they record your time and place,' said Bog, playing devil's advocate.

'Shoplifting. If you never pay, you'll remain unobserved.'

'OK. You've got an answer for everything. Did you notice that my glass is empty?'

'I've got an answer for that too!' said Alan, and he stood up and took the empty glasses to the bar to be refilled.

And that was the end of it, thought Bog.

However, two days later he got a phone call from the police. Apparently, Alan, off-his-face on illegal substances had been arrested for disturbing the peace and theft of a thousand pounds' worth of assorted items from a number of high street shops. The heroic idiot had turned a drunken conversation into a full-scale scientific experiment. Bog admired Alan for it, but thought he was foolish to try something like that in Cambridge: the city where Sir Isaac Newton had been educated and venerated. 'Never play with quantum physics in a Newtonian environment.' he moralised.

'If you follow me, I think I can help', said Jimmy.

'Thank you' said Bog, wary of the kind of help that Jimmy might give.

Jimmy led Bog out of the front doors to the main car park. Bog breathed a barely audible sigh of relief that Jimmy did not lead him to the security Portakabin, because he wasn't sure if there was any residual magnetism left in his leg and if there was, it might encourage the security guard to ask a number of awkward questions.

Instead, Jimmy led Bog through the car park and round the front of an attractive new surgery building to the less attractive rear. There, at a rakish angle, with one wheel up a kerb, and stuck between two huge refuge bins, (as if it was trying to camouflage itself as a third), was Bog's car. It had a huge yellow clamp on one of its front wheels, which Bog didn't recognise, but then again Bog didn't particularly recognise much of the car. It was only when he got closer and saw the bale of hay on the back seat that he shrugged his shoulders and said, 'Yep, that's mine.'

'Do you normally park like this?' said Jimmy with a sneer he had been taught in a two-week course called 'How to Deal with Members of the Public.'

'I don't know,' said Bog, now quite blasé, having found his car again. 'It looks strangely at home there, doesn't it? Who do I pay to get that yellow hub-cap off?'

'If the car is still here, you pay at reception. If we've got it towed away, you pay the local council at their car impound. The only reason we haven't phoned the council already is that we can't work out how they could get their pick-up truck around the bins and the no parking bollards to drag that piece of crap out of there.'

'Ah, then it will be safe for another half hour while I go and visit a patient.' said Bog. He turned to walk back to the main hospital entrance and away from James

163

Chamberlain.

Jimmy was quietly fuming and wondering how the power that he had as a hospital official had somehow been usurped by the unexpected apathy of a car owner. Bog should have been grovelling to have the wheel clamp removed by now and thanking him humbly and promising not to do it again. He hated Bog and he hated Bog's hippy friends: they just didn't react the way people should in these situations.

Michael had just finished ferrying the last lot of Bog's hippy friends to Wandlebury. He parked the car, begrudgingly paid the parking meter, (a parking meter in its natural urban habitat was OK, but here in the woods it seemed wrong in so many ways), and then he led Kelly, Lynn and Enschol Bralcht to where he had left Violet and Gavyn twenty minutes earlier.

He took them anti-clockwise, (or widdershins, as the pagan in Michael insisted), beside a bumpy fallow field that caused him to regret that Dan was not with them. He stopped the group from going further and then asked if any of them had seen Lethbridge's figures. When Kelly and Lynn said 'no', he did his best impression of Dan and told them about the history and pre-history and politics of Wandlebury.

'If you removed those trees down there and stood on that opposing hill, where we are standing would be a great green canvas. Along the South Downs, the chalky soils allowed prehistoric man to carve great white figures into their green hills as acts of worship, or veneration, or graffiti. Oh look...' he said with mock surprise, pointing at piles of white stones that clustered across the landscape. 'This is a chalk rich landscape! That coincidence and some pieces of circumstantial evidence from folk tales led a guy named T C Lethbridge to hypothesise that there were chalk figures here at Wandlebury. So he started looking for them. He'd learnt a technique that Fenlanders used for finding covered ditches, which involved forcing a heavy steel bar into the ground until you hit more compact earth and started making 'soundings'. Using this technique across this field, he found the figures he was looking for. Somehow he got enough political backing to be able to excavate a central figure of a woman on a horse, but no sooner had he revealed this giantess than the political climate changed and his work was condemned as wishful-thinking or even fraud. His figure was covered, or if you believe it was a true prehistoric figure it was 're-covered', and the conservative and closed minds of Cambridgeshire forgot all about this man-made wonder or at the very least filed it away as a 1950s archaeological folly. However...'

Michael knelt down and picked up a piece of chalk. Then, on the concrete paving, he drew a primitive picture of a woman with an owl-like head and three breasts upon a tentacle-faced horse with a bent crescent moon above her. He stood up slowly, appreciating his own artwork and with a quick 'stay there!' he ran into the centre of the lumpy field and shouted back to them, 'Here's the head, beneath me!'

He ran to another set of bumps and shouted, 'here's the horse!', and again, 'Here's the moon!'

With the chalk illustration as a guide, Kelly, Lynn and perhaps even Enschol Bralcht could indeed see the scars of Lethbridge's figure. Those mounds they had ignored as mole-hills every other time they had come to Wandlebury, (for a walk or for a seasonal ritual), they now saw as something miraculous: a giantess beneath the hill, something magical beneath the mundane, and something spiritual beneath the profane.

'Do you know the great white horse at Uffington?' wheezed Michael, having bounded back to the others. 'I was once told that if you sit and meditate upon the eye of the horse and make a wish it would come true. Now, I'm a gullible sort of guy, so I thought I'd give it a go. The problem however with these chalk figures...is the same thing that makes them incredible: the scale. You can only really appreciate them from a distance. Up close, it's just a series of white lines. Anyway, I took my bearings down at the bottom of the hill, fixed my goal in my mind's eye and started trudging up to the horse to make my wish. I got up there and sat down upon the wishing spot and, with the world seemingly beneath me and a grey drizzly heaven above me, I felt at one with nature and let my wish leave my mind and travel through my body into the very ground itself, to resonate with the spirits beneath the soil and then back up to vibrate the rain drops and echo off the low cloud. It was a magical moment.'

'Did your wish come true?' asked Kelly, interrupting the story.

'No, it didn't actually,' Michael replied. 'I can't remember what I wished for, but I do remember coming back down the hill with one eye fixed on where I was sitting and as I got further and further away from the horse, it began to dawn on me that I had missed the horse's eye by some distance and I had instead been wishing upon the old nag's knee cap.'

While Kelly, Lynn, Michael and Enschol Bralcht followed the path around the Iron Age ditch and down a steep hill to where Violet sat beneath an accommodating oak, they discussed how lucky or unlucky a wish upon a horse's knee was.

Violet sat with her eyes partially closed like a cat: relaxed but wary. Gavyn had wandered off looking for mushrooms but promised not to stray too far. Amongst the trees, in an oxygen-rich environment, with the light turning to jade or emerald through the canopy filter, she wrapped her legs into a full lotus and began to meditate. She was at peace. She was tranquil. She was at one with nature, like Michael upon his misplaced horse's eye. She stayed that way for several minutes before Lynn broke the spell with her army-booted approach and an asinine observation. 'You, look peaceful.'

'Yes, I was,' said Violet, trying hard to mask the sarcasm.

The masking worked. Violet's anger about being abruptly snatched away from her peaceful state of mind remained imperceptible to Lynn, and as Violet's anger withered the two women began to talk about meditation. They both craved knowledge about how the mind, body and spirit worked. Violet wanted to know anything that would help her to understand Buddhism, which she accepted she knew little about but found that everything she had learnt fitted so well with her innate beliefs that perhaps reincarnation existed and that this life as a Christian-baptised liberal-minded modern English woman was a sequel to some previous life of devotion in a monastery or nunnery in the Orient. Lynn wanted to know more because she had a genuine need to help people. It was an addiction. It was a reaction to the lack of help that she felt she had received in her life. It was hardly healthy: some of the people did not want helping and perhaps some did not *need* helping, but she needed to help them. Any method that could provide another tool to soothe someone's metaphorical brow or control their inner demons was of interest to Lynn.

Michael, ears alert to new theories and beliefs like a psychic radar overheard Violet talking about three 'Tan Tian' points within the body and several road maps and route plans by which energy could flow. Lynn mentioned the seven chakras of Reiki and Buddhism and Michael, dredging his mind for memories of a time he had spent hanging from a tree like a ripening fruit, added to the conversation by naming several of the energy lines. He also ignited the interest of the group, who were dedicated to self-experiment, with an off-hand mention of the debate within Taoist circles about the existence of a middle or central line through the body ('The Middle Mai'). Apparently, if it did exist no one was really sure about its purpose.

This brought in Gavyn, who had returned from his mushroom hunting with a notebook and pen under his arm. He mentioned a hymn, which he had sung at school. 'There was one particular hymn, which began with the line "God is working his purpose out..." This always troubled me.'

Some of the others were troubled by it too and remembered their own school experiences; droning atonal religious songs with minimal understanding; like mantras.

Gavyn continued. 'Does this mean that God, the Supreme Being, hasn't already planned and tested his creation? I mean, it's nice to think that free will exists and we can define our own futures, but doesn't this mean that God's been "winging it" all this time and crossing his fingers that it will all work out in the end? It's no wonder the world is the way it is!'

There was a pause while many of the group decided how much they could add to a conversation about a god they did not believe in, when Lynn, with a smirk upon her face, said 'Amen!' And the tension broke into giggles, which, in dappled sunlight beneath the trees, was one of the most magical noises imaginable.

'You don't seem to have found any mushrooms,' stated Kelly, noting Gavyn's lack of mushrooms.

'On the contrary, I found loads.' Gavyn opened up his notebook to show Kelly some rather fine pencil drawings with annotations scribbled next to them indicating colour and location and surroundings.

'You're one of these new moral hunters then?' he asked. 'The sort of person who hunts down orchids with a camera or endangered species with an electric tag and a radar gun'.

'Oh no,' confessed Gavyn. 'I'm one of the old type of hunters. I'm going to rape and pillage the countryside. I'm going to pluck the mushrooms out of the ground, fry them in butter and eat them, but I really don't know what's poisonous and what's edible at the moment, so I thought I'd find the mushrooms today, identify them tonight using books and the internet and then return someday to get my breakfast.' He looked nervously at Lynn, just in case she didn't realise that his claims at being an environmental ravager were not to be taken too seriously. 'It's OK,' he said. 'Most of the mushroom is hidden under the ground and, so long as you don't take too many, it's a sustainable crop... especially in this country where nobody picks them for fear of being poisoned.'

But Lynn was not paying too much attention. She

was trying to pinpoint a spirit; an invisible, barely tangible something that she had been sensing ever since she arrived at Wandlebury. She had detected spirits here before: the place ran riot with elemental forces and faeries and ghosts, but this one seemed closer. This one was stronger.

Chapter Nine:
The Fake in the Bath

At Addenbrookes hospital Old Dan was conscious and anxious to talk to Bog. 'Are there any others here?'

'No. I'm afraid I'm the only one today. The others are all at Wandlebury this morning.' Bog neglected to say that he was only there because he needed to find his car. 'Who's in the group now?' asked Dan, not wanting to lead Bog to any particular answer but afraid that he already knew it.

'Well, there's me and Michael and Lynn (you remember Lynn?) and a young couple called Violet and Gavyn and a strange scruffy bloke called Kelly and a quiet foreigner called Enschol Bralcht.'

'Bollocks!'

'Huh?'

'For a while I thought I was having flashbacks or was daydreaming or was just getting confused in my old age.

173

Bollocks!'

'What's wrong?'

'I used to know a man who called himself Enschol Bralcht. This was back when I was young. I think I was still at University or maybe it was a year after I'd left, but I was still hanging around with the old crowd. We were linked for a while with the Cambridge Ghost Club, the club that claimed Peter Cushing and Dennis Wheatley and the Ghost hunter Harry Price...but that's another story. We were a loose coven of free thinkers and satanic dabblers sucking up the spirit of rebellion that had been put there by the likes of Byron, and Marlowe and Crowley before us.'

'You were a bunch of over-privileged slackers having fun with your parents' money whilst you still could,' interjected Bog.

Dan ignored him. 'We were arrogant and powerful and stupid, and the most powerful and arrogant and stupid was a post-graduate called Enschol Bralcht. He had developed one of those scary personas that a lot of occultists dream of creating.'

Bog nodded in recognition.

'Young students were in frightened awe of him because his background was mysterious. He was frequently cruel to those who were younger than him and he always hinted that he knew more than any of the rest of us. I and a few of my generation, however, had a way of keeping him in check. We remembered him when he was an undergraduate.

174

We knew his real name, not that silly pan-European mystery name, but the mundane name that he was Christened with. He knew that we remembered his less mysterious youth and could reduce his proud image to dust, should we need to. A power balance was thus maintained.

'However, Enschol Bralcht was not in the coven to fit in. Even amongst the odd people who find forbidden knowledge attractive he was determined to be odder.'

Bog tried to imagine someone odder than Strange Kelly and if Dan had paused long enough in his story Bog might have commented on this to the old man.

'Whatever we believed in, he took a determined stance against it. In retrospect he provided a useful devil's advocate to our more out-of-line practices and beliefs, but at the time he was just plain obnoxious.'

'Like Kelly,' Bog said under his breath.

'I think we used his character traits against him in the end. There was a book for sale. You might still be able to find details in the local newspapers, but at the time they were redecorating the dorm where a young Edward Alexander Crowley lived whilst at Trinity College studying Moral Science. Anyway, they found this book, under the floorboards (or so the story went). This was patently a fraud. They said it was Aleister Crowley's lost grimoire. It had 'Adoleo Me' on its leather bound cover and was said to contain some of his secrets about self sacrifice. It was complete hokum. Anyone with any local history or occult knowledge knew that Crowley's university career was way before he fixed his title as 'Aleister' or his subtitle as 'The Wickedest Man in the World'. He spent far more of his youth dreaming of being a mountain climber than scaling any magical Hierarchies.

'But the more we pointed out the stupidity of the book, the more Enschol Bralcht defended it and when it finally came up at auction, the spoiled brat borrowed a large amount of money from his parents and bought it. We laughed. We laughed when he bought the book. We laughed when he said, in his serious po-faced manner, that he knew the secret of life-everlasting. Even though he had the kind of face that devoured humour, behind his back, we found him hilarious. Some of my crowd even laughed when they found out about his suicide. There were all sorts of amusing stories about how he died with a crucifix up his anus or of a heart attack mid-coitus with a goat. I didn't. I was too much involved by then. I...'

For a man who liked talking and a man who made a living from local history, Old Dan's floundering at this point in his personal history seemed peculiar. Bog didn't know whether he was supposed to interject or comment at this point. He remained silent but embarrassed.

After a long pause Old Dan regained his composure and continued. 'When I came to Michael's house, I saw him again. It could have been a relative, I guess. It could have been my imagination. It could have been a ghost; come to haunt me, but bloody hell he was there. He hadn't aged since... since I last saw him...dead. He was there. He was hanging over Michael like a bloody wraith: Enschol Bralcht...resurrected.

Both Dan and Bog were logical men. They'd seen a number of odd things in their lives, but neither was prepared to accept that they had proof of life after death without further checks. Dan asked Bog to describe 'his Enschol Bralcht' to compare with Dan's Enschol Bralcht.

Bog tried but found it difficult to describe the man's character and so moved on to describe his appearance, which was even more difficult. Enschol Bralcht had not left much of a trace in Bog's head.

Bog suggested that perhaps Enschol Bralcht was in fact Enschol Bralcht II, the son of the original Bralcht. It seemed in character with the hypothetical father that he should try to achieve immortality by repeating his name upon his theoretical offspring.

Dan again questioned his memory of events. Bog, although the younger man, questioned his own. Each tried to use cold logic to avoid the unsettling emotional scenario that Dan was an accessory to suicide and that if someone were selfish enough to take his own life to achieve power, how much more of a threat might he be to others' lives?

At Wandlebury, the pagans were sitting on some travel rugs that they had found in the back of Michael's musty, dusty squinting car. They were laying out a picnic, whilst picking at the more tasty bits. The fruit cakes, Jam sandwiches and sweet fizzy colas were predictably alluring to the local wildlife, and Violet, for one, was not happy that a persistent wasp had fallen in love with the whole display of snack foods and was showing his affection by dive-bombing the large two-legged mammals that were between it and its paramour.

Lynn was trying to describe to Kelly where the burial mounds were, but as neither of them shared any points of reference at Wandlebury, and one tree looks very much like another, they were not having a very useful conversation. Like the wasp, they were too persistent for their own good, and any normal person would have given up long before with a cursory. 'Oh, it doesn't matter. I'll show you later.'

Enschol Bralcht, on the other hand, was being less persistent. He was falling apart physically. As Gavyn noticed Enschol Bralcht's body become transparent, he wondered — rather light-headedly - whether he should not have touched one of the mushrooms he had found.

However, as the resurrectionist's body faltered, so his mind reached new strengths. Just as Michael had suggested, this place was invigorating. There was something about it that provided Bralcht with enough energy to regain lost memories and solidify his liquid plans. He knew who he was. He knew what he must do. He knew that not far away his enemy was also beginning to grow strong. With a heightened awareness of his surroundings, he also knew that he must concentrate again on keeping his body intact. He could not let the pagans suspect him. His concentration left his memory and threw its energy at the task of solidifying his body. His acute hearing, however, was providing him with an annoying distraction. Although he wasn't scared of being stung, (the thought never crossed his busy mind), like Violet he was beginning to be irritated by the buzzing of the wasp that was circling the group.

Despite eating, talking and admiring the view, everybody had some part of their attention on the wasp. Some, like Violet, were scared of getting stung and some, like Enschol Bralcht, were just distracted by the insect, but everyone was shocked at the insect's death.

From the corners of their five sets of eyes the pagans noticed the wasp perform its aerobatics with a mixture of fear and annoyance until it flew a foot or two in front of Enschol Bralcht, (who no-one had been paying much attention to, as usual). Bralcht raised his hand with the open palm to the sky. The wasp landed upon it like a trained hawk and then Enschol Bralcht closed his fingers. Everyone heard the crunching of carapace as the insect was crushed to death in Bralcht's grasp. There was no look of pain on Bralcht's face as the dying insect presumably stung its assailant. But there was no expression either of malice or triumph. Enschol Bralcht's face was cold and inscrutable as ever.

Despite the fact that no-one liked wasps at the picnic party, everyone felt strangely sorry for the creature that had died this way. They were also shocked by the matter-of-fact way in which Bralcht had performed this trick.

'How did you do that?' asked Michael.

Bralcht shrugged his shoulders and smiled his best smile yet.

Gavyn was as shocked and impressed as everyone else, but thought he knew how it had been done. Enschol Bralcht's hand must still have had strawberry jam on it from handling a sandwich. The calm manner with which he had laid his hand before the wasp was not just to show off before the audience but also so as not to scare the insect away. The wasp had then been attracted to the hand by the sweet sticky jam and whilst lapping it up, Enschol Bralcht had slowly wrapped his fingers around the insect. He must have done it in a way so that the wasp couldn't flex its abdomen upwards or downwards to sting Bralcht. It had been cleverly done, but was explainable. It must have taken a lot of antihistamine cream before Enschol Bralcht had learned how to do that without flinching.

'Didn't that hurt?' asked Lynn with genuine concern for Bralcht.

'I think it must have done', he said unemotionally, looking at the crushed body in his hand.

Bog was worried. Old Dan wasn't telling him everything, but the story that he had told about a young powerful magician obsessed with proving himself and willing to dabble with death, was making Bog reconsider some of his experiences of the last week. Dabbling with death was what got magic a bad reputation in the first place. Death magic or necromancy got corrupted to become 'negremancy', which when translated as 'black magic' enforced a morality system on something that was originally just another form of science. Now everything you do as a magician goes under the moral microscope and is judged as good or bad; white or black.

Although Bog was against such simplistic dualities, it did make sense to him that Enschol Bralcht, quietly skulking at the edges of his friends and colleagues, was evil. He hadn't seen Enschol Bralcht commit a single malevolent act, but something about him - a feeling, the sort of feelings that magicians relied on - said he was evil. 'But if that is Enschol Bralcht resurrected, why should we be worried?' Bog asked. 'What harm could he do?'

'I don't know,' Dan replied. 'Maybe he means no harm. Maybe he'll *do* no harm, but he'll certainly want to keep on living. Every young man is interested in immortality, but very few of them are prepared to kill themselves to live forever. Perhaps he's a ghost, unable to hurt the living, or perhaps he's a spirit in search of someone to haunt and draw power and life from. I'm afraid it could be the latter...I'm afraid it could be me.'

Bog was afraid it was just as likely to be him, or any one of the pagans. He realised he might just be being paranoid now, but what really worried him was that after Dan

181

had been taken to hospital Enschol Bralcht had continued to haunt Cherry Hinton. If the parasite was taking power and life from someone, then it could not be Dan. Dan had his reasons for fearing Enschol Bralcht and they were tied up in the packaging of guilt, but Bog had his reasons too.

Four months ago Bog had been at the seaside. It had been the first time he'd been to the coast since the motorcycle crash that had changed him from a biker to an ex-biker. It had been a cold and grey day. The sky had been grey and the sea had been grey and Bog's mood had been a grey melancholia. In the old days, he would have been there with a large group of bikers, laughing and joking and fighting at the edge of the world. He had forgotten how magical these places were: where the land comes to an end and you realise man's limitations. The mix of salt air, magic and melancholia had drawn him to a small booth on the ugly concrete boardwalk. Between the doughnuts shack and the chip stall was the gypsy.

It did not make sense for Bog to ask a gypsy for his fortune. He knew a number of psychics, who would have done it for free. He could even read the cards himself if he needed to. Bog however had not been feeling himself at that time. He'd been cold and it probably hadn't just been the weather that had chilled him to the bones.

He'd knocked on the door and had crossed the threshold. The gypsy had been a perfect stereotype: leather faced and bedecked in cheap gold jewellery. She'd worn a scarf upon her head like the typical pictures of gypsies suggested she ought to. She had pulled out some nicotine stained cards and had asked Bog to shuffle and cut the deck. She had asked him for £10 (a paltry sum for a future) and she had asked him to trust her. She had then arranged the cards in a semi-circle and had held his hand as she'd told him what to expect from the cold grey world outside her booth. Most of what she'd had to say had been easily forgotten: pleasantries and complements. The part that Bog now remembered with an eerie clarity, was:

'One of your friends... One of your close friends will face a serious threat before the year is out... It will come from an unexpected place... but it will be a physical threat and you will be able to help him...or her...in a physical way...if you are prepared.'

This was a threat from an unexpected place. He had been prepared. Since the fortune telling, Bog had hidden his protection in a bale of hay in the back of his four-wheeled vehicle, but he needed more proof and more of an idea how physical a threat Enschol Bralcht could be to anyone. If he was just a ghost then it was unlikely he could even harm a fly.

'If you need proof...' said Dan, 'go to St. John's. I think there's still a photo of the rowing team on the wall. Bralcht was not a very good rower but he did join us one season and I think he's probably kneeling on the front row in a group shot.'

Jimmy Chamberlain, (usually called Jimmy), and his sceptical ilk would tell you that magic was a gullible reaction to a set of coincidences. Duncan O'Connell, (usually called Bog), would tell you that it didn't matter whether you call the phenomenon 'magic' or 'coincidence': it existed and could therefore be studied, tested and experimented upon. Enschol Bralcht, (whose real name was now known to Bog), did not believe in coincidences. While Bog left Dan's bedside to go and pay for his car to be released from the wheel-lock, Enschol Bralcht borrowed the keys for Michael's car in order to fetch the map-book from the glove compartment.

Enschol Bralcht told Michael that he wanted the map for research reasons. Michael, now used to filling in the details that Enschol Bralcht left unfilled, thought that he was looking for the coordinates of the burial mounds on the ordinance survey map. Lynn had dragged the group to meditate and feel the power emanating from these old structures, and Michael was unsure whether one small hillock was any older or more powerful than another. He was especially wary of meditating upon the wrong mound after his experience at Uffington.

Enschol Bralcht, on the other hand, was not interested in the burial mounds. Death did not interest him. So while Lynn led Gavyn, Violet, Kelly and Michael to the mounds, he sat himself in the warm depression that had previously housed a peaceful Violet, folded the map out in front of him and concentrated. The map was not just a paper representation of reality; the map was sympathetic to reality. The smaller scale universe that lay upon Enschol Bralcht's lap was, in his mind, inseparable from its full-scale cousin. His eyes bore down on the part of the map marked 'Addenbrookes Hsp' and refocused until, despite the limitations of the mapmaker's art, he could see the individual buildings and then the individual wards and then the people in the wards, and Dan and Bog both scurrying about the map like microscopic paper mites. The universe and the representation of the universe were one.

Bog, (the real full-scale version and his tiny avatar), had just got into his car, and with a number of backward and forward movements, and plenty of gear-crunching, had managed to extricate it from the alleyway where he'd abandoned it the day before. Bog's plans were now as fluid as Michael's. He didn't know what he was going to do beyond finding proof that Enschol Bralcht was or was not a malevolent spirit. He had a lot of strange beliefs and like Michael and the rest of the pagan community, he collected sophisms, but he was also a practical man and refused any mental leap until he was sure of his landing.

Bog was not a happy man behind the wheel of a car and he was thus easily distracted. He was travelling directly into Cambridge when he suddenly found himself in the wrong lane. Instead of continuing past the railway station and into the town centre, he awoke from a dark forgetful fog to find himself on Cherry Hinton Road heading back to Cherry

Hinton. He cursed himself out aloud. He was, after all, a magnanimous driver and was as prepared to shout abuse at himself, as he was to any other cyclist, motorist or naïve pedestrian who wandered into the road in front of him.

When Bog realised that he was going the wrong way, he was faced with a decision: he could either go back the way he'd come or turn right along Queen Edith's Way to get back to Addenbrookes in order to start the journey again. Bog decided to turn right. Why was a road named after Queen Edith? Who was Queen Edith? There was a part of Bog that wished that Dan were there with him to answer these historical questions: perhaps that was why he was now heading back to the hospital.

Dan was perceptive. He had not been fully conscious for long and his mind was still picking up all kinds of information and analysing it indiscriminately. He was daydreaming. One of these specific flights of fantasy centred on Bog, who Dan saw as a driver of a car, with Enschol Bralcht as his passenger. Enschol Bralcht was smiling a calm dull smile from behind a map-book and was calling out directions to the driver.

Most normal people would dismiss this image as a burst of random subconscious nonsense: a 'brain-fart', as Bog would call it. Most normal people, lying weak and old in a hospital bed, would not divide their energies into two separate areas. Dan was not normal. He had been not normal for longer than anyone could remember. He had stood weeping at the funerals of his normal friends and had absorbed the special history of his city until its quirks were his own. He therefore took notice of Bog's journey in his daydream, just as Enschol Bralcht took notice of the journey on his sympathetic map.

Dan summoned the energy within him that he called magic and placed it in an imaginary miniature version of himself, no bigger than his head. He projected the little Dan towards Bog's car until (in his mind) it sat upon the dashboard like a plastic Jesus. He wished it well, imbued it with as much of his strength and personality as he could bear to lose and said goodbye. He was now free to reverse the damage he had done many years before, when he had foolishly helped Enschol Bralcht kill himself.

Fifty years ago, Dan had received a letter from Enschol Bralcht. The relationship between the two men had been an odd one. Dan had thought Bralcht was a pretentious idiot, (a fairly common form of wildlife, native to Cambridge University). He'd thought Bralcht had had a lot of talent for magic but that did not give him an excuse to be an arrogant and abusive arse. Bralcht had frankly been an embarrassment. However the more forgiving parts of Dan's heart and head had thought that, given time, Enschol Bralcht might mellow: he might stop trying to prove himself and start being himself instead. Dan had thought that Enschol Bralcht in return had hated him. The letter however had suggested otherwise.

The letter had hinted that although Enschol Bralcht did not like Dan, he'd thought he was trustworthy and talented. It had been a letter to a respected enemy. The letter had also been, in summary, a suicide note. However, suicide notes are usually written in despair and contain simple requests for forgiveness from those left behind. This one had been a statement of intent. It had laid out Enschol Bralcht's plans for self-sacrifice, and his requests for Dan's help, in meticulous detail. This was to be a ritual death and Enschol Bralcht needed it to be perfect.

Dan and his coven had talked about life, death and the wonders and horrors in-between, but seldom had they dabbled in any magical practices beyond the odd seasonal rituals. The letter, however, had been serious and Dan had not wanted a part of it. With the letter and its contents, (a pair of white evening gloves and an ornate-handled knife), stuffed into his coat pocket, he had run out of the house, jumped onto his bicycle, (then, as now, the only way to get across Cambridge with any speed), and had headed to St. John's College. His intention had been to give Enschol Bralcht a good slap and to tell him that he wanted no part in Bralcht's silly little drama.

Enschol Bralcht had been a talented and intelligent magician. He had left no room for fate, the gods or Dan to ruin his serious and perfect practice. By the time Dan had cycled across Cambridge, run across the college campus from its porter's lodge across the river and to Enschol Bralcht's tower-top dorm, Enschol Bralcht's part of the plan had already been completed. The red-brown bathwater had been cooling, the blood flow had begun to slow, and the body had been still.

Dan had knocked on the door. There had been no answer. He'd paused a long pause, (for an impatient man, fuelled by anger and exercise), and then had turned the handle and let himself in. Despite the letter's insistence, Dan had not worn the enclosed gloves when he'd entered the room. At that point he hadn't thought he'd had to. Only once he was inside had he reconsidered his plan to slap some sense into Enschol Bralcht. There had been a smell of wet fur and faeces. There had been a stillness in the room; light from the window had revealed dust motes sitting stagnant in the air. There had been an absence of sound and there had been a feeling in a corner of Dan's mind that had sent the hairs on the back of his neck into attention and had held his heart in a moment of paralysis.

Beneath the dust haloed window was a table that should have been used for studying textbooks. Instead it had held three wet corpses: a rabbit, a pigeon and a cat. The rabbit and pigeon had been nameless residents of the grasslands that bordered the River Cam. The cat had been called Aristotle. It had been a much-fed stray, adopted and pampered on scraps from first-years' lunches. It had gone missing three days ago. The animals had had their limbs

189

slashed and had been held in warm water until they had bled to death. They had either been votive offerings to the gods of death or practice sacrifices to ensure that the main event had gone smoothly. Enschol Bralcht had killed them as if they were nothing. They had been insignificant. They had been insects.

Dan had surprised himself by his calmness. This had been the first time he had seen anything like this or had been in a situation like this. He'd had nothing to compare it with, but had still been surprised at the unflinching way that he'd returned to the door, put on the gloves and had cleaned his fingerprints from the door-handle. Perhaps Enschol Bralcht had seen within Dan the same calmness and unemotional traits that he prided within himself. Perhaps Bralcht had been Dan's twisted mirror. Dan had been analysing his actions for fifty years and he did not like some of the conclusions that he had reached.

Once Dan had cleaned his prints from the door he had re-entered the room and closed the door carefully and quietly behind him. Then he'd walked to the bathroom to find the body. He'd known the body would be there because all of this had been detailed in the letter. He had known that he was too late to save the arrogant young man. He had known that he and his friends were partially responsible for driving Enschol Bralcht to more and more ludicrous acts, by their disapproval. He knew had known that he was fulfilling Bralcht's last will and testament and that not following

Bralcht's instructions would have felt like a final betrayal and would make the man's death even more pointless and stupid. This had been his reasoning when he'd entered the bathroom and had pulled out the ornate-handled knife.

Dan had been instructed to swap his knife with its twin; the one that had killed Enschol Bralcht. Dan had looked around the room. The knife had been supposed to be there: on the floor where the dying man would have dropped it having carved gashes along his wrists to let the blood out. There had been an empty bottle of aspirin on the floor, but no knife. Dan had raised his glance from the floor to the body. Again, he'd been surprised at how calm he was about seeing a dead body. However, the body had been just a thing. Without the spark of life within it, a human body is no more frightening than a door handle. This hadn't been just some philosophic argument of Dan's; this was what it really had been like. The body had seemed fake: like a real body but paler and less life-like. Dan had still been young enough then to find death fascinating. He had stared at the body for a while.

Enschol Bralcht had stepped into the bath without a shirt on, or socks, but to preserve his modesty he'd worn a pair of jeans. Dan had found this faintly amusing. When he'd been a child it had been the fashion for people to buy jeans a little too big for them and shrink them by bathing in them. Somewhere, in heaven, hell or elsewhere the spirit of Enschol Bralcht would be looking smart in a pair of nicely

191

fitted denim trousers.

'Bollocks', Dan had said, quietly but still audibly. He had seen the knife. Enschol Bralcht had completed one last trick on his most respected enemy: he had dropped the knife inside the bath, rather than outside upon the floor.

Dan had taken off one of the gloves and reached down into the bloodbath. There had been no one there to see him, but still he had grimaced in disgust as he brushed past the body and pulled the knife from the bloody water. 'You Bastard', he'd said in a whisper.

He'd put the wet knife in a plastic bag and then back into his pocket. He'd let its twin sink back into the bathtub to rest more or less where the other one had lain. He'd then left the room the way he had found it and had cycled the long journey to the Gog Magog Hills where, on the dead man's instructions, he had buried the blade.

Now, fifty years later, wracked with guilt and regret, Dan would have to go to the Wandlebury mound and undo the magic that he had set in motion. He would have to dig up the blade and remove Bralcht's link to the place and its spiritual power. One thing that Dan, bedecked in a pair of pyjamas and tired due to drugs and his recent heart attack, was sure of: this time he would not be cycling.

Chapter Ten:
The Man in the Ladies' Coat

Bog was cursing the cyclists on Long Road. What were these idiots doing, riding so far from the city centre? Why were they riding three abreast? Did they not know how fed up Bog was, having already driven in a big circle due to a momentary lapse of concentration? Did they not think that their selfish abuse of the Queen's Highway might lead him to another slight lapse of concentration as he ran the idiots down? Luckily, they weaved from the road and onto the pavement like the unpredictable turn of a shoal of fish keen to confuse a potential predator, and Bog was able to get past and turn onto Trumpington Road, which became Trumpington Street, central Cambridge.

Trumpington Street is Cambridge's most amusing street: it has the usual shoals of erratic cyclists, it has its share of architectural distractions, (in the form of the great classical

193

columns of the Fitzwilliam Museum: a budget-sized British Museum for a town that breathed borrowed culture), and it had Hobson's conduit.

Hobson's conduit was Thomas Hobson's (1544?-1631) answer to Cambridge's shortage of drinking water. It was a diverted stream from natural springs to the South West of the city. Along Trumpington Street, the water was carried in open gutters beside the road: six-inch deep mini aqueducts echoing the classical styled museum. The locals could entertain themselves for hours on end, watching unsuspecting drivers accidentally putting their vehicles in these urban ditches and then scraping the bottom of their cars trying to extract them. The sound of graunching gears and the rasping of metal upon concrete was one of the two favourite sounds of Cambridge inhabitants. The other, (also water related), was the cacophony of apologies from inexperienced punters as they crashed into each other on hot summer days on the Cam. Cambridge was a city with a superiority complex and the sound of incompetence made it smile.

Bog turned right at the Pitt Building, (named after Prime Minister Pitt the Younger, 1759 — 1806), and onto Pembroke Street, (known as Downing Street at its other end for no apparent reason). He was shocked at how much Cambridge history he knew. It was if a little voice in his head was guiding him through the town. For instance, on his right, he knew that the new museums were the site of the old

Cavendish laboratories where Rutherford had discovered the atom and Watson and Crick had unravelled the secrets of DNA. Then there was the ugly new Holiday Inn Hotel, which had replaced the old lab where Maurice Wilkes had built something called 'The EDSAC Computer' in the 1940s. Bog was deep in 'Science Country' now: no wonder the pagan Bog needed a guide.

When Downing Street hit Regent Street, Bog turned right and inhaled deeply like a diver emerging from deep water. He had emerged from dark, narrow asphyxiating science into a more spiritual region of the city: buildings by the Masonic Christopher Wren, colleges built from usurped priories, an arts cinema, pubs and restaurants and a park. He turned left again onto Gonville Place where he reached the Roman Catholic Church, which, as a non-Christian Bog (and Dan) had always admired for its morbid fascination with death. It was soot-blackened and flying-buttressed to look like a charred rib-cage. The building was dedicated to holy martyrs and a trip inside would reveal in gory detail, from every stained-glass window, all the wonderful ways that you could die for your god.

Bog had no intention of dying for anyone today. His mission was to get to St. John's to prove a theory that was slowly emerging in his head, and perhaps save a life.

Assuming that Bog found evidence at St. John's College to back up his theory that Enschol Bralcht had come back from the dead, the next question was 'why?' Dan had been sure that Bralcht was back to haunt him for some past indiscretion. Bog doubted this. Enschol Bralcht was not haunting Addenbrookes Hospital. Enschol Bralcht was haunting Michael's group of pagans. He was always there; lurking quietly in the corner. None of them had ever met Bralcht during his life, so why was he interested in them now, during his death? Bog thought that it must be to gain power from the group, but how and for what purpose he did not know. What he did know, (in his heart, if not in the logical scientific organ he kept in his skull), was that the gypsy's prediction was reaching its moment of fulfilment: one of his friends was going to need his help.

It didn't matter how anxious Bog was now feeling, he could not make the traffic go any faster. There was a trick mentioned in a Chaos Magic book he'd once read, involving the conjuring up of an avatar called Goflowolfog, but although this autonomous thought-form seemed to help change the traffic lights, it had little effect on the sheer volume of traffic that was trying to nudge its way around the streets of Cambridge.

The traffic crawled past the Grafton centre, Cambridge's sterile and characterless mall, (the sibling of identical shopping complexes around the country), and as road rage crept in, Bog got forced once again into the wrong lane. If he were honest with himself, he would have to admit that he wasn't paying attention. A black cloud like a welcoming darkness for the sleep-deprived hit him at the point when he should have been pulling off to the left hand lane, and instead he had to cross over the roundabout and over the River Cam and round another stretch of inner ring road before he could cut into the city to get to the college.

As he drove over the Elizabeth Way Bridge he daydreamed about abandoning his car there and then, and taking the direct route to St. John's: over the side of the bridge into the river and a twenty minute swim. In a hot metal box on heat-absorbent black tarmac, within a haze of car exhaust fumes, a cool swim seemed so very inviting. Bog cursed himself for missing his turn again. He did not like being in a car any longer than he had to.

In a cool breeze, beneath a rustling tree, Enschol Bralcht sat smiling intently at the map of Cambridge. Here at Wandlebury, he had newfound strength and purpose and was happy to prove it, moving a microscopic bug across the paper. His hand involuntarily opened and closed as if he still held a struggling wasp. If he hadn't been enjoying this so much, he might have noticed that his enemy was coming to Wandlebury and he might have been able to stop him.

Dan's first obstacle was his clothing. He was wearing some night clothes that the hospital had provided and although it had been very generous of the National Health Service to provide him with such fashionable and practical pieces of nylon and string, he could not walk out of the hospital doors

197

for fear of being arrested for exposure. His eyes fell upon the young woman sitting on a chair next to her elderly father in the next bed. Over the back of the chair lay her light tan trench coat.

There are two types of magic. There's the magic that some people do not believe in: a magic akin to miracle, but without the need for a god. This magic involves an understanding of symbols and the knowledge that this physical universe is a more complex structure than logic alone can describe. Then there's the other type of magic. This magic involves stages and audiences, top hats and bunny rabbits, cards and smoke and mirrors. This magic involves a basic knowledge of psychology and the ability to make the impossible appear possible, despite an audience's logic. Aleister Crowley misspelt one of these magics to stop the two being confused with each other. He needn't have bothered. In practical situations, such as stealing a coat from someone, there is a will and an action, and whether the woman was distracted by Dan's misdirection skills or whether the fairies stole the coat from the back of her chair while she wasn't looking, doesn't matter. These are just two of many interpretations of the fact that Dan was now walking down the hospital corridors wearing a stolen trench coat, just long enough to cover up his drafty night clothes.

From Elizabeth way, Bog took the first exit off the roundabout and headed down Chesterton Road. This ran parallel to the river and so long as he didn't get stuck in the wrong lane again he could now turn down Victoria Avenue and drive past Midsummer Common, (with its single street lamp standing in the middle of a cattle strewn field: looking as odd and incongruous as the lamppost-and-satyr combination in the Narnia books that C.S. Lewis wrote while at Cambridge).

Of course, the black mist descended again and Bog missed this turning, but it was a close thing. Bog's surprising knowledge of the geography of Cambridge kept his route fixed in his mind and he would have taken the left turn to Midsummer Common if it hadn't been for a serious and sudden muscle spasm that jerked the steering wheel and changed the direction of his car. Bog was starting to believe that something was preventing him from getting to St. John's. It was as if there were two passengers in the car with him arguing about which way he should go. With the back seats taken up by a bale of hay, there was only one spare seat in the car, so it was no wonder these two other beings were antagonistic.

Bog was now passing the Castle Mound on his right (obscured by buildings) and Bridge Street on his left. If Bridge Street wasn't blocked off by bollards it would have provided the simplest and quickest route to St. John's, but the town planners and the black mist were working in unison now and Bog drove through this area (the Old Jewry of 13th Cambridge) with only a cursory pause at the traffic lights to get to the area of Cambridge known as The Backs.

The Backs is an area filled by the backsides of the colleges as they sidle up to the river. It's the 'picture postcard view' of Cambridge with straw-hatted punters passing before great architecture to provide an image of an unchanging England for tourists to take back to their countries and dream about. It is a clean and grassy fake. There are no tramps. There is no industry. There are not even many students as they are encouraged not to lounge too close to the cameras to spoil the view. The Backs are what the city wants its tourists to see. It is in fact a front!

Bog passed this area and turned up Fen Causeway to get back to Gonville Place and East Road to begin his lap of Cambridge once again. The road name would be a peculiar one, if it were not in Cambridge. There was a Fen Causeway, a Maid's Causeway and a Worts Causeway. They denoted a time when only the occasional raised path could cross the expanses of wetlands that surrounded the city. Cambridge was a water-based city, built on water-trade, (run by the old Jews of Bridge Street), with the remnants of ditches, dykes and conduits from many centuries trying to get fresh water into the city and dirty water out. This was England's Venice: old and damp and plague-ridden. There was even a Bridge of Sighs, built upon Venetian design and situated in the grounds of St. John's College. This image reminded Bog of his destination and despite the presence of a black fog at the back of his mind he was determined not to do another lap of

Cambridge: he would reach St.John's College and find out the truth behind Enschol Bralcht.

Dan had reached the front doors of Addenbrookes when he was hit by a revelation. He was a liberated man. When you are young, you have the idiocy of youth and think you are invulnerable to disease, impervious to pain and immune to the law. Only now did he realise that stealing a stranger's coat was only the beginning. Only the old were immune to the law. If he were caught committing some sort of crime, what would the police, the judge or the jury do about an octogenarian recovering from a heart complaint? The police would let him off with a warning, the judge would pronounce him too ill to stand trial or the jury would be sympathetic to the old rogue. Dan had made up his mind; to thwart a ghost and save his soul from the burden of guilt he would steal a car to get to Wandlebury.

Having discarded his previous moral and legal objections, Dan took to crime like a natural and looked at the vista before him with glee. There were vehicles everywhere: doctors cars, and ambulances left with doors ajar and engines running while patients were helped into Accident and Emergency. There were cars abandoned by their owners because they couldn't find a legitimate parking space and needed to rush a relative into hospital without delay, and there were council vehicles full of tools and debris, while workmen filled holes in the road, rearranged flower-beds or painted new and confusing road markings on roads already sodden with yellow and white paint.

Bog was driving past the Grafton Centre for the second time in an hour, but this time he was concentrating on taking the Newmarket Road turning and heading West towards the college. He thought of horses (Newmarket was 'The Home of Horse Racing'). He thought of water (Newmarket Road became Maid's Causeway after a few hundred yards). He thought of Midsummer Common (inner-city grazing land that he would be passing on his right, if he took the correct turning). This seemed to help.

Bog's will was strong now. He was still wary, but there was less chance of him losing concentration now he was so close. He soothed his fragile ego by deciding that a journey round Cambridge widdershins was probably not just a mistake, but it was also a very pagan thing to do. In fact, he reasoned, it should probably be regarded as an essential ritual to placate the great and cruel road-gods who ruled over Cambridge in conjunction with the twins (not Gog and Magog, but 'Town' and 'Gown': the conflicting Civilians and Academics).

Bog went straight over the next roundabout and found himself on Jesus Lane. A voice from inside his car and inside his head told him that he was passing Sidney Sussex College on his left, where Oliver Cromwell's head was buried in a secret location, (to avoid this secular relic being dug up and used as a rallying point for Republicans). Bog remembered when he and Alan had bluffed their way into the chapel a few years ago, where with a pair of dowsing rods they had located the burial place. It had been fairly obvious and hadn't involved much psychic talent at all. The head had practically glowed with hatred as The Lord Protector's role in English and world history had been assured when he'd taken the head of the King of England and had turned international politics upside down.

As Bog turned right, he looked up at the building in front of him. It was just another collegiate building: old and yellowed like a tooth. It did however offer some proof of the validity of Feng Shui and its insistence that being at the end of a long straight road was unlucky. There, at the end of Jesus Lane, was the only damage that Cambridge had received in World War II: a couple of bullet hole cavities in the old tooth; a present from a passing German aircraft, its pilot bored on his way back from Coventry or some-other more important strategic target.

To the right, Bog could just see the Round Church: one of only four Templar built temples left in Britain. It was round because it was built upon the design of the Holy Sepulchre in Jerusalem. The later standard of cruciform churches had no biblical blueprint, but probably came to prominence as Christians tried to distance themselves from their Jewish forbears.

And to the left was St. John's College.

203

Bog had intended to get to St. John's in a hurried twenty minutes. It had instead taken him an hour and he still hadn't figured out where he was going to park. He'd driven as fast as he could but it hadn't helped: a bit like a bat out of hell, if the hell ring-road was snarled up at rush hour and a large lorry full of brimstone had overturned causing a 4 hour delay on the Northbound carriage-way. A rogue memory bubbled up from the depths of Bog's mind to the surface. A long time ago, he had thought of a great plan for parking in Cambridge, which he had never been desperate enough to use until now. He pulled up right in front of the College and slammed on his breaks, scaring a ragged flock of pigeons and a slightly smarter flock of tourists. This was just one of the many places in the city where parking was strictly forbidden. He then removed from his vehicle a large yellow and black sign that, some months before, he had acquired from an abandoned car. It said 'Police Aware' and its identical copies were put in the windows of cars that had been stolen and subsequently located by the police. The police manpower situation was such that with one of these notices in your car window, it would ensure you four days' free parking before the police came and towed the vehicle back to their compound to dust it for finger prints and identify its owner.

Before Bog abandoned his four-wheeled vehicle, he smashed a small side-window and two of the indicator lights, just to make its theft look more realistic. The feeling of complete contentment that accompanied this act of violence was overwhelming and almost made the ex-biker cry. Here was a revelation: the feeling that he had had for his four-wheeled vehicle, that for so long he'd thought was ambivalence, was in fact hatred. He hated this vehicle with a passion that only a biker can have for car. He smashed another side window in joy. He hoped his bale of hay would be safe on the back seat. He was beginning to suspect he might need it.

Chapter Eleven:
Digging Up Roots

In Wandlebury, Enschol Bralcht was not happy. Michael and the others had come back from their burial mound meditation and had noisily disturbed his game of cartomancy and mind control. Before they ruined his concentration, he had become convinced that the little driver in the little car travelling along his map was being protected by an unseen force and had decided that instead of slowing his journey by making him take the wrong roads, he would instead make him swerve into the approaching traffic. The resulting crash should have not just slowed Bog's journey, but stopped it altogether.

But now this would not happen and Bralcht cheered himself up with the thought that no matter what Bog found out at St. John's College, he would be too late to thwart the resurrectionist's plans. For a newcomer to human emotions,

Enschol Bralcht was getting the hang of them very quickly.

The pagans swept Enschol Bralcht up into their chattering throng and continued to the car park and Michael's old car. Bralcht had no option but to go with them. They had decided that it was a foolish waste of petrol to make two trips back to the house and so with Lynn in the front passenger seat and Violet sitting on Gavyn's lap to make room for Kelly, and Bralcht in the back, he was forced to fold up the cumbrous map and let his mind come back to his body.

As the car pulled out across the road and back towards Cambridge, Bralcht remembered the last time he made this journey with Tom Hypolite and Bob Marley. He was so much stronger now; he was not fading out of existence as much as he had at the beginning of the week. Soon, he would have a permanent body and then he would have proved to himself that he was immortal. The bodies might die but he could move on. He could possess anyone he wished, commit ritual suicide and then move on: always one step ahead of death's scythe.

As Enschol Bralcht gloated in the comfortable but snug back seat of Michael's executive toy, he did not notice his enemy passing him on the other side of the road. Old Dan, his mind split between Bog's destination and his own destiny, was also not aware of the importance of that moment. He did however note that the car, with its one working headlight, did appear to be winking at him as he passed.

To be fair to Dan, he had only recently come out of hospital and had never driven a council maintenance lorry before. Its gears groaned when he used them. It smelt of stale cigarettes and was littered with paper work as its cab was used as an office, whilst the flatbed backend held the shovels, picks and lumps of concrete that represented the workmen's current project. 'Beggars can't be choosers,' said Dan to himself, classifying his himself as a 'beggar' rather than the more accurate but less complimentary 'thief.

He swerved into the car park and realising what sort of vehicle he was driving he smiled at the parking meter as he drove past it. His lorry looked like it was supposed to be there. It looked like it was probably used by workmen who had come to Wandlebury to repair the paths, cut down overhanging trees or dredge the pond. In fact, this innocent appearance might also extend to his own activities. He reached behind the passenger seat and pulled out a workman's reflective yellow waistcoat. He put it on, got out of the cab and selected a spade from the back of the lorry. He was right: at a distance he looked like a workman and it was only when you got up close you realised that workmen were usually younger, usually wore shoes and seldom wore lady's trench coats beneath their reflective yellow waistcoats. On the back of the waistcoat was the logo 'Cambridge Council' in large dark authoritative letters. No one would question a typeface as municipal as that.

He found the blade with relative ease. Guilt, (the feeling that he was responsible for something evil), had kept the location fixed in his subconscious. The trick with burying items in a wooded area is not to mark their plot by trees. Trees are too impermanent: they grow, they die, they fall down, and over the decades you might even be forgiven for thinking that they move. Dan had instead remembered the blade's sacred burial place by trigonometry with the troll-bridge over the old moat and with the scarcely hidden foundations of a Victorian greenhouse or shed.

After five minutes of scrabbling around in the dirt with the spade and then with his more dextrous bare hands, he found the remains of the plastic bag and its partially rusted content: the blade made sacred with the blood of Enschol Bralcht. It was Dan's job, (duty, responsibility or quest), to undo the damage he had done when he had complied with Enschol Bralcht's suicide note, all those years ago. It was Dan's job to sap the resurrectionist's power, to sever his link with the sacred power of a sacred item buried in a sacred place. Dan needed to find a new resting place for the blade; a place so mundane that not even the greatest psycho-geographer or antiquarian could link it with power, man-made or natural.

This was more difficult than it at first seemed. Dan knew Cambridge better than most of its transient occupants and knew that its associated history and learning meant that every square foot of earth could be linked to a great writer, great scientist, historical event or accumulated feeling of importance.

'Outside the city, then.' His words escaped his mouth as a quiet breeze through the woods. 'In a Boggy Fen? The soil black as Enschol Bralcht's intent?'

But no, the fens were not just soil; they were the soul of Cambridgeshire. They were what separated it as a region from every other London Commuter Zone. Local pubs, which along with churches formed the hearts and identities of the fen villages, had walls full of sepia photographs of the last 'Drains', when the rich land that had been reclaimed from the sea had been rereclaimed by floodwater upon a biblical scale. In some pubs, there were also flat, rusted and rustic skates and perhaps even a picture of young Dan in a scarf and deerstalker hat; fen-skating, as old Fenlanders were apt to do, when the February freeze turned the boggy fields to glass.

So Dan could not desecrate the blade in the city nor the countryside.

'What's left? Destroy it in acid?'

No, despite some contacts in university chemistry departments, he could not get enough acid to do the trick, nor did he have enough time to wait for a bone handle and steel blade to waste away.

'Destroy it in fire?'

Well he could sneak it back to Addenbrookes and bury

it amongst the bio-waste to be incinerated onsite, but giving the blade a Viking funeral surrounded by body-parts and bad tissue, to rise up Addenbrookes' chimney, (the tallest structure in Cambridge), and infect the very clouds themselves, seemed to give Enschol Bralcht more power and not less. No, it had to be an unconsecrated burial in a nowhere place of no power nor importance, so that the monster's dark roots could no longer feed from rich soil.

'That's it!' Dan shouted, scattering woodpigeons from nearby trees. He threw the blade into his bag and with the energy afforded to an old man by a Eureka-moment, he stood up, and at a military pace made his way back to Wandlebury's car park, to his vehicle and his new destination.

Having spent so long reaching his destination, Bog was now unsure of what his next course of action should be. He had come for proof that Dan's story of a young necromancer called Bralcht was true, but had no idea how to obtain this information. There are three ways that a person can achieve their goals: through natural ability, through experience and through luck. Although Bog had watched his fair share of police programmes on TV, he suspected that he was not a gifted detective. He also had no experience of the university; how it was run and to who you could go for information. He did however have magic on his side. Luck in the form of a sigil, freshly written in spit upon his chest, went with him into the college.

'...Oh yes,' agreed the porter, taking Bog across the Bridge of Sighs. 'The Norton Dominator was one hell of a bike. I never had one myself, but a mate of mine used to own one and I had a go on it once. The best I could ever afford was a Kawasaki Ninja: a totally different kind of ride. Great fun, but a tad dangerous. Of course, then I got married and had some kids and the bikes gave way to more sensible four-wheeled vehicles...'

And Bog and the porter both sighed a sympathetic and synchronised sigh.

Echoes followed Bog and the porter down the academic corridors as they continued their nostalgic evaluation of the history of motorcycles. Their echoes bounced off the walls and continued to ripple towards the Cam, even when the two figures had turned a corner and were out of sight. The echoes finally caught up with them on the second floor of a dormitory block, where the plain monastic-whitewashed walls were suddenly decorated in a garish abundance of photographs. These were the rowing team pictures: one taken every year since the annual boat race with Oxford University began in 1854. Bog ran his eyes across each photograph looking for a face that he only partially remembered: the forgettable Mr Bralcht.

Dan was on the road again. He had a plan. He remembered

213

all those old ghost stories and folk tales that he'd been told as a child. When an evil man was killed, or a monster or an enemy, their body would not be buried in a churchyard to be at peace, nor anywhere else where it might find some strength to claw its way back to haunt you. They were always buried at crossroads: places between places, places with no identity of their own, their markers not pointing to heaven but to a confusing choice of earthly locations, nowhere places. This was where the blade should be buried.

Dan knew of the perfect location. He drove north, meandering through the outskirts of Cambridge until he hit the A14. Then he travelled a couple of junctions west, until he found what he wanted, and pulled off the road onto the hard shoulder where only broken-down cars, emergency vehicles or council trucks doing maintenance work were allowed to stray.

The road planners of Cambridgeshire are an unnaturally dull lot. They have little imagination and if an idea is proved to be successful in one area, they tend to repeat it ad nauseam. Thus, to the north west of the city you can turn off the A14 travelling west and join a new road going north. This new road is also called the A14. If you wish, you can travel a few miles further north to Huntingdon, (following the trail of the Jews when they were 'asked to leave' Cambridge in 1275), where you can again turn off the A14 and join a third road called the same.

Dan did not have to drive that far, (and he suspected

214

that he was running out of time), so he got out of his cab, picked up his favourite spade and the most hated blade and climbed over the barriers to get to some exhaust-blasted, soulless, litter-covered, oil-soaked barren land to perform his desanctifying ritual.

The ritual was brief and unelaborate: a long and elaborate one would show respect to the blade and thus be counter-productive. He took the blade in his hands to break it. He was however an old man and his strength was not enough to accomplish this task. He tried bending it. But the blade was a fine and expensive one, (as best befitted its owner: a rather spoilt university educated brat), and would not bend. Dan dropped the blade and concentrated on the spade. The soil was hard and crumbling; its nutrients and soft vegetation leeched from it by chemical abuse from the road. It took some effort to dig a shallow grave, but no one stopped Dan. Presumably, the police were now looking for a delusional Addenbrookes patient in a stolen council maintenance truck, but the passengers of the hundreds of cars that drove past noticed only a lone workman completing some non-specific work.

When Dan had finished digging his shallow grave, he kicked the knife into it and then opening his borrowed trench coat, and lifting his hospital smock, he finally completed his desecration act by pissing on the blade: old man's piss, dark and pungent. He then covered the ground over it and stood back to examine his work. He was pleased: the disturbed earth looked as poor and barren as the surrounding land. There was nothing to show what was buried here. There was no shrine and somewhere a monster must be losing its strength.

Bog was also pleased. His neck was straining from looking up at so many almost identical photographs of groups of almost identical young men with crossed oars in front of them, (reminding Bog faintly of the crossed bones of a pirate flag), but he had finally found what he was looking for. There before him was a thumbprint sized face of a young man that looked almost identical to the man who called himself Enschol Bralcht. He was smiling in a way that seemed unnatural even then, and beneath the picture were the names of all the rowers, including the very normal boring British name that Enschol Bralcht had been Christened with: the name that Dan had known and had used to hold the pretentious young magician in check.

Bog's standard emotional reaction to life was to be gruffly and moodily amused by things: friendly but miserable. Michael always thought that Bog reminded him a little of Eeyore, A.A.Milne's moody donkey from 'Winnie the Pooh', but hadn't told anyone this — especially not Bog.

Bog now had to fight a rush of contradictory feelings that his stable, logical and mechanical mind was unused to: happiness that he had found what he was looking for, wonder at the fact that he now possessed irrefutable proof of the afterlife, and horror that if Dan's story was true then his friends were now in danger from a being that could not (or would not) die.

Bog thanked the porter as much as he could in the little time he had available and rushed back down the stairs, through the corridors and across the Bridge of Sighs to get back to his car. He followed the echoes of his motorcycling conversation like breadcrumbs through a maze.

He got to his car without a hitch and since it was the only car sitting on the pedestrian only area, surrounded by small frostings of broken glass and labelled 'Police Aware', for once he identified it quickly and without any doubt. He did however drive a few yards towards Trinity College, (the college next door to St. John's where A.A.Milne had been educated), before he realised that he was going the wrong way and turned the vehicle round. Dumb flocks of tourists and pigeons still tried their hardest to get run over but fate, luck or some other pagan deity ensured that Bog left St. John's with no blood on his wheels.

Bog's new plan was a simple one, and if a black cloud had drifted into his head, (which it didn't), it still would not have distracted him. The plan had been there since his encounter with the fortune-telling gypsy. He had been told that he would need to help a friend in a real and physical way and so there in the back of his car was a real and physical tool for helping people. Like many of his pagan friends he did own a magic wand, which was a device for focusing his willpower into a point or a beam. In the back of his car, however, was a bale of hay, which hid a mundane wand within it. The mundane wand was too big to fit in the car's glove box, which is why he hid it in a bale of hay. It was about three and a half feet long, had two barrels, a custom made hardwood stock, and a hair-trigger held in check by a safety catch. Bog was hunting monsters.

In the house at Cherry Hinton, Michael was making tea for his guests: a very normal suburban activity. In the front room, his guests were tidying up and discussing an exorcism ritual. Throughout the journey, Enschol Bralcht had been surprisingly animated about this ritual and insistent that it be completed soon. Now, back at the house, he was once again his quiet inconspicuous self, as if something had suddenly sapped the energy and life from him.

Comparing the notebooks of Michael, Gavyn, Kelly and Enschol Bralcht, the group was surprised at how similar the ideas were in each of them, (with the exception of Bralcht's notes, which were non-existent but for a swirly doodle). They all seemed to hit upon the idea of using string magic. Violet even humoured poor Enschol Bralcht, (whose English, it was supposed, was not good enough to write magical notes), by suggesting that the swirly pattern on his pages represented a ball of string and was therefore an unconscious agreement with the others. The synchronicity of the researchers was seen as a good omen for the ritual's success.

Gavyn, the most scientific minded of the group, asked if string magic had anything to do with string theory. It was a question asked with some humour but he regretted it as soon as it escaped from his mouth, as Lynn used it as an excuse to detail the practice. She explained that it was the use of string as a symbol of magical willpower and the colour of the string was important and comparable to the colours of your chakras. The whole practice could be mixed with numerology as a number of knots could be made to symbolise things and cause effects.

'Like the symbolic knots of Christian monks' belts,' Gavyn said with a straight face.

'Like the knot languages of the Inca people,' Lynn countered, quickly and aggressively.

Luckily, at that point, Michael came back into the room with a tray full of teas, preventing Gavyn from mischievously aggravating Lynn's biases further.

'In my opinion, string magic is the opposite of string theory,' Michael opined. 'String theory is a perennially fashionable piece of theoretical physics used to try to get to the physicists' Holy Grail: The Universal Theory of Everything. It's what old Cambridge natural philosophers and mathematicians like Newton were searching for, ever since the Church stopped burning them for their thoughts. String magic, on the other hand, is one specific tool in the larger arsenal of magic. The Universal Theory of Magic is that a strong enough belief that something will happen will make it happen. What tools you use to help you believe - wands, robes, candles, bits of string or other believers - all help, but if your belief is strong enough you don't actually need all the rituals and paraphernalia.'

'What a great advert for the forthcoming exorcism ritual!' said Gavyn with a light-hearted sarcasm.

'Well, I was hoping to wait for Bog before we started.'

'But we must start soon,' said Kelly, in a tone and urgency that were not entirely his own.

'OK,' Michael said. 'How about we get everything ready now and by the time we've set up the ceremonial circle he'll probably be back. Let me finish my tea and then I'll wander over to the corner shop for supplies. We'll see what happens next.' Michael had learnt his lesson about making plans and intended to use the 'see what happens next' mantra with increased frequency in the future.

The tea was hot and there was a strange atmosphere in the front room, as each of the pagans in turn was visited by an anxiety to get on with the ritual. There was however no arguing with the laws of physics and the obstinate tea took its time to cool, unmoved by the unspoken pleas of the drinkers.

'What colour string do we need?' asked Michael with a façade of relaxed indifference.

'Red,' said Kelly and Lynn in unison.

'Red for the passion: for the new life and vitality you

need to cultivate,' said Kelly.

'Red for the root chakra: for the grounding to a fresh reality without a spirit on your back,' said Lynn.

'Red for luck (in China),' said Violet.

'Red for power,' whispered Enschol Bralcht.

'Er...red for strawberry?' said Gavyn, feeling that he had to contribute something to the conversation.

'You know, if we were to wait for Bog to return,' said Michael, ignoring Gavyn's contribution, 'he's got some bright orangey-red baling twine wrapped around that bale of hay on the back seat of his car. We could use that?'

'No. We should not prevaricate any longer' said Enschol Bralcht, firmly.

'...and besides the orange colour is more associated with the sacral chakra or belly chakra, which is more to do with sex,' said Lynn. 'You weren't having any sexual problems with your wife, were you?' She watched Michael's face turn red with embarrassment.

Once everyone had finished their tea, Michael went to the corner shop to buy some string. The fresh air felt good upon his face and he inhaled deeply. The atmosphere in his front room seemed to be getting a little oppressive for him: he couldn't help but feel that he was being bullied into a rushed ritual, and Michael felt uncomfortable about rushing anything in his life. He was old enough and wise enough to know that life continued at its own pace and that impatience leads to stress, which speeds up nothing but your own funeral. It was with such a cheery image in his head that he entered the corner shop and searched the aisles of assorted junk for red string.

Eventually he found some cotton sewing-thread. The thread was finer than he was looking for but he consoled himself with the old homily: beggars can't be choosers. For some reason he was overcome with a feeling of déjà vu, but as he couldn't remember what part of this scenario seemed so familiar he could do nothing but wipe the irritating feeling from his mind and pay for the thread - and of course some incense sticks, which the shopkeeper insisted that he needed. Michael wondered whether the Asian shopkeeper was insinuating that his smell was offensive and needed masking by incense. He'd once heard, from an Indian friend of his, that all Europeans smelt a little like wet chicken. This was a typical example of Michael's fickle and fact-filled mind: two minutes ago he was thinking of funerals and now he was pondering racial stereotyping and chickens.

Tom Hypolite was continuing his own project in racial auto-stereotyping. He was travelling in a 'beat-up' car, trailing exhaust and marijuana fumes, whilst a reggae compilation screamed peaceful and laid-back shouts at him and anyone unfortunate to be within two hundred yards of the vehicle. He was driving through Cherry Hinton on the way from his college to his affordable accommodation, (many miles outside the city centre), when his foot, so relaxed by the throbbing Jamaican beat, fell asleep and slipped from the brake pedal. His concentration lapsed for only a second, but it was long enough for his car to crash into the car in front. The collision was slower than ten miles and hour, (as both cars had been crawling along in the sluggish Cambridge traffic), but the noise of the crunch could be heard above the sound of Caribbean music and when Tom got out of his car he saw that both rear indicator lights and some side windows of the car in front had been shattered by the impact.

Bog was not happy. He was only two hundred yards away from the house and some ass-hole had crashed into him. He was furious. The veins in his neck - not the pale tattoo marks but the real blood filled ones - stood out as the pressure of his anger turned his head 'warning sign' red. He stormed out of the vehicle with lightning in his eyes and thunder in his voice.

'You idiot, you complete idiot! Look what you've done! Just look what you've done!'

Tom had extracted himself from his car and had an anguished look on his face. No matter how much he was saying 'no worries,' to himself and to the tattooed bulldog that was ranting in front of him, he was not a laid back Jamaican beach-bum. He was a middle-class English student and he had just wrecked his only means of transport and was about to have his face beaten to a bloody pulp by a Neanderthal in a leather jacket. 'No worries... th... there's no worries... no worries...' The tape was looped. The record stuck and the CD was jumping.

'You complete ass-hole! Look what you did to my vehicle! You've destroyed it... it's destroyed... its...' The storm in Bog's head suddenly dissipated, with not even a puddle left to show its passing. He suddenly realised what he had said and smiled. Two or three seconds passed in silence, then:

'Yeah, no worries,' said Bog in a shockingly cheery voice. He turned and opened the crumpled back door of his hated vehicle to take out the bale of hay. He reached into the hay with a large fist and pulled out a double-barrelled shotgun, which he hid as best he could in his jacket before continuing his journey to Michael's house on foot.

Behind him, the normally crawling Cambridge traffic had slowed to oozing magma speed as one lane of the road was blocked by two broken cars, a scattered bale of hay and a confused nervous wreck in a green, black, yellow and red T-shirt muttering 'no worries' to himself over and over again.

Bog stormed up the street with purpose written across him like a billboard. As he came to Michael's house, he could hear the muttering of an incantation: no clearly audible words but the rhythmic chant of half a dozen people. He came to Michael's doorstep and did not stop: he kept walking and in one fluid movement raised his leg up to a goose-step and kicked the door open, breaking the latch and lock with an explosive crack.

Michael ran to the door, followed motion-for-motion and step-for-step by Enschol Bralcht: two men with one mind.

Enschol Bralcht had no choice in the matter. Even if you did not believe in magic and denied that Enschol Bralcht and Michael were linked spiritually, Bralcht was still chained to Michael physically, as he had been engaged in the act of wrapping a red cord around Michael's body three times and still held both ends of the thread.

It is easy to persuade people that an act of possession, (binding a spirit to a body), is in fact a banishing spell for binding an ex-wife from spiritually harming her ex-husband. The chants are similar, the candles and ceremony identical, only the string is not usually wrapped around the haunted party and not usually by a malevolent spirit with a willpower strong enough to reach beyond the grave.

Michael met Bog in the hallway.

'Get out, ya bastard!' Bog screamed and punctuated his demand by pulling the shotgun's trigger, releasing a sound that dwarfed that of the door being kicked in. This was exorcism, Bog-style.

Michael flew backwards past Enschol Bralcht, yanking the cords from the resurrectionist's hands as he went and landed in a rag-doll heap upon the stairway. His expression of shock and confusion was mirrored on the face of Enschol Bralcht, who now stood to accept the second blast of Bog's onslaught. The Bralcht body didn't crumple though. The two

225

shots, (three if you count the sound of the door being broken), resounded in the narrow passage and set Enschol Bralcht's clothes fluttering in a sonic wind, but the body did not fall. Fresh holes in the stomach oozed a liquid, but it was a slow and dark flood, more like treacle than what was coming from the burst damn of Michael's flesh.

Bog had rehearsed these moments in his head while driving and his actions were fast and sure. He ran up to the Bralcht body and kicked it to the floor in a similar manner to the way he had opened the door. Next, he reached over his friend Michael and unwrapped the red cord from around his chest. Now with the cord in his hands the rehearsed and unemotional Bog was leaping over the body of the evil resurrectionist, to find Kelly in the other room. Unfortunately the rehearsed and unemotional Bog only existed in ideaspace, and it was the very real, very angry and very upset Bog who stood in the hallway having just shot his friend in the stomach with a shotgun. It was this Bog who now bent down and spent an anguished few seconds ripping apart the body of Enschol Bralcht with his bare hands.

This was not a Bacchanalian orgy of blood and passion. This was not a gory 'Jack The Ripper' scene. The Bralcht body was an impressive construct of will but was not quite what it should have been: it was after all a temporary vessel for poor Enschol Bralcht. The body looked real but it pulled apart like clumps of candyfloss. Enschol Bralcht was reminded of the Entropy Room where the furniture looked substantial but was made from insubstantial balsa wood and indeed, Bog was feeling better with each handful that he ripped apart this fleshy furniture.

Happy though he was pulling apart a dead man's dream, Bog soon remembered his purpose and, praying that he was not too late, ran into the front room. There he found Kelly in a post meditative state: drowsy as a hedgehog in Spring. He wrapped the cord around the strange little man and shouted, 'Here, ya bastard!' to no one in particular and to the shock of Violet, Gavyn and Lynn. He stood there for a couple of seconds that passed like racing snails, before he saw something in Kelly's eyes that satisfied him. Then he returned to check up on bleeding Michael.

Michael had ceased to care. He felt strangely removed from his body: not a 'flying at ceiling level, oh look, there's me down there' out-of-body-experience', but the dislocation and detachment of someone in the throes of violent and terminal apathy. He watched the blood stain growing on his shirt and imagined that with the right force of will he could affect its Rorschach patterning. If he concentrated on his stomach muscles, or the properties of the shirt material, or the blood chemistry, he could form a perfect red-brown circle from it, like a red sun rising from the trousered horizon.

Then he looked up from his leaking wounds and saw the world. He saw foreground and background melt into a white nothingness. The only items his eyes could focus on were the people, the pagan-souls, the very forces of nature that Enschol Bralcht, the enemy, could see. There was Thor, the thundering short god before him, shouting lightning: Mjolnir, his hammer, still smouldered in his storm-casting hands. Thor was angry and bristling with electric anger like blue tattoos and his indecipherable words were carved into the air like runes in ice. To the left hand side of him was a collection of souls masquerading as human, but Michael could finally see beyond this. He saw Gavyn and Violet as 'The Lovers' card of the Tarot; the number six, a preternatural digit, hung over their heads like a halo. He sniggered a schoolboy snigger at their 'Adam and Eve' nakedness and noticed with ambivalence that he had no sexual feelings for either the female or male form. He saw a Lynn-faced sphinx next to them, but looking entirely in his direction through a wall that he couldn't see but knew was there in the material plain that he no longer was part of. The Lynn-sphinx's ears grew pointed and the face became more feline as word-play became reality and she became a Lynx. She pawed the ground that was not ground in front of her and curled up to sleep with eyes slit open on look-out and a purr erupting from her chest that made ripples in his vision. Nearest still to Michael was a horse with a feather boa around its neck. Michael thought that the fact that this did not seem in the least bit odd to him probably meant something, although he could not think what: he was in the deepest depths of apathy and not even a pony in party clothes could upset him, and besides, it wasn't a feather boa, the feathers were pinions of a pair of elaborate wings. He was sitting on stairs that weren't there, next to a winged horse. The horse however was not a really a horse but a black chess piece, a knight. Around its neck was a scaled boa — a real snake. The snake's head was human but indescribable. This was every snake that Michael had ever seen. This was Cleopatra's asp, Hermes' Caduceus, Hissing Sid, the Mushhushshu, the Naga, Quezecoatl, Glycon, Zmei Gorymich and the Devil-laid-low-upon-his-belly. This was knowledge beyond morals, in serpentine form, making a nest in the chess knight's head like an eel at home in coral caverns. The knight was in pain and opened its mouth to scream and the scream came out like a word and the word was 'Whombaddidley'. Michael knew exactly what was going on. He knew what had happened and what would happen and he had no power or inclination to stop it.

Chapter Twelve:
Epicentre Epilogue

Michael had been saved but was now bleeding profusely over the hallway. Enschol Bralcht had disappeared, (run away in fright or dissolved into broken pieces of nothingness?), and Kelly was twitching in an epileptic attack on the floor. Some might argue that Bog had benevolently attempted to restrain him for his own good, with the red thread that had previously been wrapped around Michael. Although the thread was just fine sewing cotton, for some reason Kelly's thrashing limbs could not break it. This was what everyone else saw and would tell the police. Michael did not mention the screaming horse, the snake, the thunder-god, the lynx or The Lovers.

'...and that's the truth of it,' said Dan in punctuation.

The moot was held every first Thursday in the month in whichever pub was regarded as the most pagan-friendly at the time. The members of the moot were all relatively young:

231

Cambridge's population has a fast turnover of individuals. Cambridge is just another way station for London, which is the true siren for any weirdos who wish to make a career out of their weirdness. The exception to the rule was Old Dan, who seemed old enough to single-handedly counter-balance the youth in the room. Everyone treated Dan with respect or awe. He had, after all, been living in Cambridge for at least sixty years, (a conservative guess), and had seen and performed all manner of strange magical practices.

However, magic will always have a large proportion of bluff about it, as magicians strut and boast in order for lesser magicians to believe in them and thus give them, in some psychological way, their power. Some of the pagans at the moot therefore doubted the veracity of Dan's story.

Occasionally, Michael and Lynn would come to the moots. They seemed to be quite close now, after Michael's time in hospital when Lynn had visited him every day. It was true that he'd spent a month in Addenbrookes recovering from a shotgun blast to the stomach. It was also true that Bog, Michael's friend, was the one who shot him and despite the police's best attempts at persuading Michael to press charges, Michael stood by his friend. Bog was sentenced with the menial charge of 'disturbing the peace' and ordered to pay a small fine. The police would have liked to put Bog in prison: gun crime is a serious issue. However, Bog had a licence for the shotgun, and of the two victims, one refused to press charges and there was no evidence that the other one (Enschol Bralcht) had even existed. They toyed with the idea that 'The Fellowship of Cambridge Pagans' was a front for an illegal immigrant smuggling organisation and searched for Bralcht's details through Interpol but this investigation came to nothing. A similar unlikely connection with the theft of council lorry by a confused Addenbrookes patient also proved to lead nowhere. The patient was 'not in his right mind' following a heart attack and eventually gave the lorry back. He had even filled it up with petrol and paid to have it cleaned as an act of repentance.

No-one could ask Violet or Gavyn about the truth of this tale as contrary to the normal movements of Cambridge residents towards London, they had instead moved further north and away from this incident.

Some pagans had tried to question Kelly about it, but Kelly had changed. He had become a true local character, like Marigold - the man who walked around Norwich with a pair of rubber gloves on, directing the traffic. Kelly still sat on a park bench on Midsummer Common, talking to himself, but now it seemed as if he could hear less and less of the outside world and his conversations with himself seemed more animated, as if he were arguing with another personality inside his head.

Printed in the United Kingdom
by Lightning Source UK Ltd.
115845UKS00001B/316-321